PROJECT:
Raising Faith

faiThGirLz!

girls of 622 HarborView

PROJECT: Raising Faith

Melody Carlson

ZONDERkidz

ZONDERVAN.com/
AUTHORTRACKER
follow your favorite authors

Project: *Raising Faith*
Copyright © 2008 by Melody Carlson

Requests for information should be addressed to:
Zonderkidz, *Grand Rapids, Michigan 49530*

Library of Congress Cataloging-in-Publication Data: Applied for
ISBN 978-0-310-71349-4

Editor: Barbara Scott
Art direction and design: Merit Alderink
Interior composition: Carlos Eluterio Estrada

Printed in the United States of America

08 09 10 11 12 • 5 4 3 2 1

So we fix our eyes not on what is seen, but what is unseen. For what is seen is temporary, but what is unseen is eternal.

— 2 Corinthians 4:18

"A ski trip!" Morgan controlled herself from jumping up and down in the church parking lot. "This is gonna be totally awesome, Emily."

Emily frowned. "Yeah, for some kids."

"What do you mean?"

"I mean I can't afford to go."

"But Cory said there would be ways to earn money."

Emily just shook her head. "I don't think he meant the cost for the whole trip, Morgan. Besides we're supposed to put down a fifty dollar deposit. There's no way I can do that."

"Where's your faith, Emily?"

"Not in my pocketbook, that's for sure."

"You know what I mean. Why can't you just trust God to provide?" asked Morgan.

"I try to trust him to provide for most things ... but a ski trip? Well, that might be pushing it."

"You think it's too big for God?" Morgan twisted a beaded braid between her fingers as she studied her best friend's expression.

"Well, maybe not too big for God ... maybe it's just too big for me," said Emily.

"Come on," urged Morgan, "don't give up just like that. You can at least ask God whether or not he wants you to go, Emily."

Emily nodded. "Yeah, I guess you're right."

"If it makes you feel any better, I don't have enough money to go either."

"Enough money for what?" asked Mom as she and Grandma joined the girls by the car.

"The youth group is taking a ski trip, including snow-boarding and skiing," said Morgan.

"When is that?" asked Grandma.

"It's more than a month away," explained Morgan. "Not until after Christmas."

"How much?" asked Mom as she unlocked the car.

"Two hundred dollars!" exclaimed Emily.

"Goodness," said Grandma. "That's a lot."

"But it includes everything," said Morgan. "Transportation, equipment rental, lift tickets, food, and everything for three whole days! Janna said it would cost more if we weren't going as a group."

"That's probably true," said Mom as they piled into the car. "Lift tickets alone are pretty expensive."

"And the church is offering ways for kids to earn money to go," continued Morgan.

"Like what?" asked Mom.

"We can make stuff to sell at the bazaar."

"That's less than two weeks from now," said Grandma.

"And Cory and Janna are going to cut down Christmas trees to sell. We can help with that too," said Morgan.

"And wreath making," added Emily in a slightly flat voice.

"Sounds like you girls are going to be busy," said Grandma.

"Does that mean I can go?" asked Morgan.

"I guess so," said Mom, "if you're sure you can earn the money. You know that things are kind of tight right now."

"I know," Morgan assured her. "And I plan on trusting God to provide."

"How about you, Emily?" asked Grandma.

"You mean, am I trusting God too?" Emily sighed.

Grandma laughed. "Oh, I know you're trusting God, sweetheart. But how about the ski trip — are you planning on going too?"

"I don't know … that's a lot of money."

"But our God is a big God," Morgan reminded her. "We can expect big things from him."

"How many kids are going?" asked Mom.

"I don't know," admitted Morgan. "But Cory said we could invite friends from outside of church. We're going to invite Carlie, Amy, and Chelsea."

"We are?" Emily's brow creased. "Since when?"

"Since now," said Morgan. "Or when we get home. We have a meeting today at two."

"And you're inviting them to go on the ski trip?" asked Emily.

"Of course," said Morgan. "How much fun would it be without them?"

"Well, I hope you have fun without me."

"Oh, Emily, don't be so negative."

"And don't be so bossy, Morgan," warned Mom. "Emily needs to talk to her mom about this before she commits to anything."

"I know …" Morgan told herself to calm down. "It's just that I'm so excited about it. It's going to be so cool."

"You barely know how to ski," Mom reminded her.

"Janna said she'd give ski lessons. And Cory said he'd teach kids to snowboard. We can pick whichever one we want, but we have to tell them when we sign up."

"When do you sign up?" asked Mom.

"As soon as possible," said Morgan.

"As soon as God provides some of us with fifty dollars," added Emily.

"Fifty dollars?" echoed Grandma.

"Yeah, that's the deposit," explained Morgan. "I have fifteen now, Mom. If you loan me the rest, I can pay you back as soon as I earn it. And I already have some bead necklaces to sell at the bazaar."

"We'll talk about it at home, Morgan."

Morgan turned to Emily. "You *are* going on this ski trip, Em. I can just feel it. God wants to show you that he is a lot bigger than you think."

"God owns the cattle on a thousand hills," said Grandma. "And a whole lot more, Emily. Morgan is right. If God wants you to go, he will provide."

"What's your family doing for Thanksgiving this week, Emily?" asked Mom as she turned into Harbor View Mobile-Home Court.

"Nothing that I know of," said Emily as she reached for her bag.

"Why don't you come to our house for dinner?" said Grandma.

"Yeah," agreed Morgan. "Grandma makes the best pies, and her cornbread stuffing is awesome."

"That's a great idea," said Mom as she pulled in front of Emily's house. "We'd love to have you join us."

"I'll check with my mom," said Emily as she opened the door. Then she thanked them for the ride and got out.

Morgan felt a small wave of guilt as she watched Emily slowly walking toward her house. She could tell that Emily was discouraged, and Morgan hoped that she hadn't come on too strong about the ski trip. Two hundred dollars really was a lot of money; and it probably did seem overwhelming to Emily. Especially this time of year when things slowed down at the resort where Emily's mom worked. Finances might be tougher than usual for their family. Still, Morgan felt certain that the money dilemma would be resolved—the girls would work hard and God would help them. She just needed to convince Emily.

"Go easy on Emily, Morgan," said Mom as she pulled into their driveway.

"What do you mean?"

"I mean there's a chance that Emily's mom won't want her to go on that ski trip. Lisa told me just the other day that she was thinking about getting a second job during the winter."

"But Emily and I can earn our money, Mom. We can make things and sell Christmas trees and whatever it takes."

"Lisa might need Emily to help out more at home," said Mom in a slightly warning tone. "I just don't want you to put too much pressure on Emily."

"But she has to go on the ski trip," insisted Morgan. "It wouldn't be the same without her."

"That's not for you to say, sweetheart," said Grandma. "But if you pray about it, maybe God will make a way for Emily to go."

Morgan just nodded as they walked up to the house. But sometimes she wondered why other people didn't have the same kind of faith she had — the kind of faith where you were willing to stand up and speak out. At least she thought it was faith — she hoped it was faith. And, unless God showed her otherwise, she'd continue to believe that it was faith. In the meantime, she'd be praying really hard for Emily to go on the ski trip.

Morgan went to her room and started going through her bead box. Her beading supplies were a little low at the moment. She had several necklaces partially done, as well as enough beads to create a bracelet or two. Still, even if she sold all of them, it would probably be barely enough to cover her deposit and certainly not enough for Emily too. Besides that, the church bazaar was almost two weeks away — what if the ski trip filled up before then? What else could she do to earn money?

She looked around her room. She had some sewing projects going, but they weren't the sorts of things you could sell at a bazaar. She also had some watercolor paintings that she'd been working on, but she wasn't so sure that anyone would want to buy them. She wasn't even sure she'd be willing to have them hanging on a wall for people to gawk at. Art was still a somewhat personal thing to her.

"Morgan," called Grandma. "Come eat lunch." As they were eating, Morgan told Mom and Grandma that she was short on beads and was wondering if there was anything else she could make to sell at the bazaar.

"I'm knitting things for the bazaar," said Grandma. "But it takes time to knit."

"And I'm not a fast knitter at all," said Morgan, but she didn't admit that she really didn't like to knit. She didn't want to hurt Grandma's feelings.

"I have an idea," said Grandma as they were finishing up. "You could make socks."

Morgan frowned. "Socks? You mean by knitting?"

"No. I got a sewing pattern in the mail a couple of months ago. It's for polar fleece socks."

Morgan brightened. "Like for skiing and snow and stuff?"

"Yes, I suppose ..." said Grandma. "Generally, I thought they'd be for keeping your feet warm."

"Weren't you going to make some of those to sell in my shop?" asked Mom.

"Yes, but I just haven't gotten around to it."

"Do they look hard to make?" asked Morgan.

"No, I don't think so. They may involve a bit of cutting. But the sewing looked like it would be simple enough ... if you follow the directions." Grandma winked at Morgan.

"I can follow directions," said Morgan as she set down her milk glass. "It's just that I sometimes like doing things *my way.*"

"Well, that works for some projects, but I suspect the socks need to be sewn a particular way."

"Can I try making some?"

"Of course. I even have a bit of polar fleece for you to practice on. It's that tiger stripe that's leftover from the throw I made for your room."

"Cool."

"No," said Grandma. *"Warm."*

"Right." Morgan thanked Grandma for lunch as well as the sock idea then looked up at the kitchen clock. "I gotta go unlock the clubhouse before the others get there," she said as she stood. "I want to invite everyone to the ski trip."

"Just remember," said Mom. "Two hundred dollars is a lot of money. Don't make anyone feel bad if they can't afford to go."

Morgan gave her mom a wounded expression. *"Mom,"* she said, "I would *never* do that. They're my friends. I don't want them to feel bad. I just want them to have enough faith so that we can all go and have a really awesome time."

Grandma laughed. "Don't worry, Cleo," she said to her daughter as Morgan headed for the front door. "I think Morgan has enough faith for all five of those girls."

"That may be so," called Mom. "But, Morgan, it's a deluge out there. Put on your rain slicker before you go out. I don't think you have enough faith to stay dry in that downpour."

Morgan grabbed her bright orange slicker and went outside. Mom was right. There was a regular monsoon going on. She stood on the porch for a moment, just watching the rain careening down the gutters like waterfalls. She peered across the way to Emily's house, also shrouded in rain. In need of paint and some other repairs, Emily's house was the most rundown of the mobile homes in their park. But then Emily's mom was only renting and couldn't afford to fix it up much. Morgan knew that Mrs. Adams didn't get any child support and had a hard time making ends meet. Then there was Carlie's family on the other side of the beach trail. Their house was in better shape, but only because Mr. Garcia was a hard worker. Still, with their three kids to support, Morgan knew that it probably wasn't easy for them either. Maybe Mom and Grandma were right. Maybe it was silly of Morgan to think that all the girls in their club could afford to go on the ski trip with her. The truth was Morgan wasn't even sure that she could earn two hundred dollars in a month's time. Maybe it was just a crazy notion.

Then Morgan thought about what time of year it was — late November. She usually made gifts for her family

and friends during December. What if she was so busy trying to earn money for a ski trip that she had nothing to give?
Wasn't it selfish to think only of herself right now? All these
troubling thoughts ran through her mind as she jogged down
the sandy beach trail, jumping over pond-sized puddles, as she
made her way to the old bus that served as their clubhouse.
Even as she turned the key on the door of the beloved rainbow bus, she didn't feel a bit encouraged — instead of its usual
bright and cheerful colors, thanks to the gray clouds, the bus
looked dull and dowdy today. Then, just as Morgan stepped
on the stair to go inside, a whoosh of rainwater slid off the
sloped roof and splashed down onto her head.

　　She shuddered and went inside, closing the door behind
her. She peeled off her coat and dried off her glasses. Maybe
it was the gloomy weather, or maybe it was her mother's
warnings, but it suddenly felt as if Morgan's faith was shrinking — and shrinking fast.

chapter two

"Let's call this meeting to order," said Morgan as the girls all chattered away as usual. Their wet raincoats were piled up at the front of the bus, and the insides of the windows were already steamed up from all the moisture. Morgan had turned on the little heater as well as the strings of colorful lights that she'd gotten at the gift show last summer, but even this didn't seem to be lifting her spirits. Emily, the secretary, went over the minutes of their last meeting, which, as usual, took just a couple of minutes. Then Amy said she had an announcement.

"Miss McPhearson has invited us to her house for a post-Thanksgiving tea," said Amy with her usual authority. "She'd like us to join her at three o'clock on the Saturday following Thanksgiving. Does that work for everyone?"

"Not me," said Chelsea. "Our family is going on a ski trip for Thanksgiving. I'll be gone until Sunday."

"Lucky duck," said Amy.

"That's not all," said Chelsea. "I just found out that my dad got me a really great new snowboard. He was going to save it till Christmas, but Mom said that he'll probably let me have it early and—"

"*You* know how to snowboard?" asked Carlie.

"Mostly I know how to ski," said Chelsea. "But my brother promised to teach me, and he's a really good rider."

"What's a rider?" asked Carlie.

"A snowboarder, silly," said Chelsea. "You didn't know that?"

"Maybe …" Carlie shrugged. "I guess I might've forgot or something."

"Well, speaking of skiing and snowboarding," said Emily. "Morgan was going to tell —"

"Wait a minute," yelled Amy. "I'm not done with *my* business yet. I need to know who can go to Miss McPhearson's house for tea." She glared at the girls. "Hands, please."

Morgan, Carlie, and Emily raised their hands.

"Thank you." Amy pushed a strand of black hair away from her eyes. "I will let Miss McPhearson know ASAP."

"Okay," said Emily, "Morgan wanted to —"

"Wait a minute," demanded Amy again. "You haven't asked for the treasurer's report."

"Oh, yeah," said Emily. She rolled her eyes. "I'm sure it's changed a lot since last week."

"It's proper procedure," said Amy. Then she read the amount in the treasury fund and frowned. "I was thinking we should either start having dues or do something to earn money."

"Why?" asked Emily.

"In case something comes up," said Amy. "Like when we did the park project. It would've helped us to get started if we'd had a little more cash on hand."

"But it worked out," said Carlie.

"I know," said Amy. "But as a responsible treasurer, I feel it's my duty to encourage our club to be financially fiscal."

"Financially fiscal?" Morgan frowned at Amy. "What do you mean? We're not a business."

"We're sort of like a business."

"Oh, Amy," said Chelsea. "Give it a rest, will ya?"

"Yeah," agreed Emily. "Now Morgan has something to tell us." Emily turned and looked at Morgan.

"Oh, I don't know …" Morgan wasn't sure she wanted to make her announcement now.

"What's wrong?" asked Emily. "I thought you were going to invite everyone —"

"I don't know if it's such a good idea now." Morgan tried to give Emily a look — a look that was supposed to say "I don't want to talk about this now." But Emily obviously wasn't getting it.

"Hey," said Chelsea. "What's the deal, Morgan? First you're going to invite us to something, and then you change your mind and un-invite us?"

"That's not very polite," added Amy.

"Yeah," said Carlie. "What's up with that, Morgan?"

"Fine, fine," said Morgan, holding up her hands. "I'll tell you. I was going to ask everyone here if you wanted to go on a ski trip with our youth group. It's the week after Christmas, it's for three days and —"

"All right!" said Carlie, giving Chelsea a high five. "I'm in."

"Me too," said Chelsea. "I can't wait to show you guys my new board."

"I'd like to come too," said Amy. "I've never skied before, but I'd like to try."

"How about you, Emily?" asked Carlie. "You're coming too, right?"

Emily looked down at her lap. "I don't know ..."

"Why not?" demanded Amy.

Emily looked up now, her eyes on Morgan. "Tell them," she said. "Tell them how much it costs."

"Well, I was about to ..." Morgan adjusted her glasses and looked at her friends. "But then I got interrupted. Anyway, the trip, which includes transportation, lift tickets, equipment rental, food, and lodging ... is two hundred dollars."

"That's not bad," said Chelsea. "Count me in."

"Whoa," said Carlie. "I don't know about that ..."

"It's a good deal," said Chelsea. "Seriously, I heard my mom saying how much our weekend is costing us — trust me, two hundred dollars a person is not bad."

"Maybe for you," said Carlie. "But I don't have that kind of money."

"Two hundred dollars?" said Amy in a thoughtful voice.

"Yeah," said Morgan. "Is that too much for you too?"

"No …" Amy slowly shook her head. "I think I can afford that. My parents have been paying me for helping in the restaurant lately. And I'll work a lot during the holidays. Plus, tips are supposed to be good during December. I'll go."

"Not me," said Carlie sadly.

"So, I'm not so sure," said Morgan. "I've been having second thoughts about the whole thing. Maybe we should make some kind of pact. Either we all go, or none of us go."

"That's not fair," said Amy.

"Well, I don't know if I want to go …" began Morgan. "I mean, if Emily and Carlie can't go too. It just wouldn't feel right to me. It wouldn't be fun. Maybe we should just forget it."

"Wait," said Emily. "You didn't tell them everything, Morgan." She turned to Carlie now. "Our church has ways for kids to earn money."

"But I don't go to your church," said Carlie.

"I don't think that matters," said Emily. "The youth pastor said we could invite our friends." Then she told the others about the Christmas bazaar and selling Christmas trees and wreathes.

"Really?" said Carlie hopefully. "We could do that?"

"But two hundred dollars is a lot of money," Morgan pointed out. "And there's not much time. And anyone who goes needs to pay a deposit of fifty dollars, and I'm guessing that needs to be paid pretty soon. Plus, don't forget it's Christmas ... it can get pretty busy, you know."

Carlie frowned. "Maybe you're right ... maybe I better not try to do this."

"Hang on," said Emily. "You can't give up that easily."

Morgan stared at her friend in surprise. "But I didn't think you were going to go, Emily."

"I never said that."

"But you worried about the cost."

"Yeah, and you kept telling me to have bigger faith. What happened to your faith, Morgan?"

Morgan blinked. "I still have it. I just didn't want to be too pushy ... in case some of us couldn't go."

"Well, I'm not ready to give up," said Emily with a stubborn smile.

"Really?" Morgan felt a trickle of hope again.

"Me neither," said Carlie. "I might even see if I can do some babysitting for my mom again. There's a whole week of no school right before Christmas. My mom might pay me to watch my little brothers so that she can get some things done before Christmas."

"So, it's settled?" asked Morgan, still feeling surprised.

"Everyone who wants to go on the ski trip, raise your hand," said Amy.

Everyone's hand, except Morgan's, shot into the air. Then Morgan sheepishly raised her own hand.

"This is going to be so cool," said Carlie. "I can't wait."

"I'll get the sign-up forms for everyone tomorrow," said Morgan. "I'll bring them to the clubhouse after school."

"When do we pay our deposit?" asked Amy.

Morgan considered this. "I guess whenever you can."

"I'll bring a check for the whole thing tomorrow," said Chelsea.

Morgan nodded. "Okay ..." But even as she said this, she wondered whether the check could be refunded if things didn't work out. Cory hadn't said anything about that. But it might be pretty weird if Chelsea was the only one to come up with the full payment for the ski trip — and she had to go all by herself. Of course, Chelsea would probably refuse to go alone. And her parents probably wouldn't even care if she didn't get her money back. Morgan couldn't imagine how it would feel to be that rich.

"Will boys be there?" asked Chelsea suddenly.

"Boys?" Morgan considered this. "Well, yeah, sure. The youth group is both guys and girls."

"What are we going to wear?" asked Carlie. And that's when Chelsea started giving them fashion tips on winter wear.

"I'll bring some magazines," said Chelsea. "That'll give you guys some ideas of what's cool right now and what's not."

"That reminds me," said Morgan. "My grandma has a pattern for socks."

"Huh?" said Chelsea.

"Polar socks," continued Morgan. "We can sew them and sell them at the bazaar."

Chelsea frowned. "You're going to *sew* socks?"

"Yeah, I think so," said Morgan. "I'm going to experiment with it. See how long it takes, how much the fabric costs … and if it seems profitable or not."

"Hey, I'm not too proud to sew socks," said Emily.

"Me neither," said Carlie.

Chelsea shrugged. "It might even be fun."

"I don't know," said Amy. "I think I better stick with waiting tables for now."

"I'll practice with the sock pattern," said Morgan. "And if it works, we can set up a workshop here at the bus. The church bazaar is less than two weeks away. We don't have any time to waste."

"Speaking of two weeks from now," said Chelsea. "My dad told me to see if you guys want to be in the Christmas parade."

"Doing what?" asked Amy with suspicion.

"Just riding on the bank float," said Chelsea, and then she giggled. "Dressed as elves."

"Elves?" Carlie frowned. "Like tights and pointy shoes?"

"Yeah. Dad will provide the costumes."

"I think it sounds like fun," said Morgan. "I'll volunteer to be an elf."

"What about the church bazaar?" asked Emily. "Isn't it the same day?"

"I don't think we actually have to be at the bazaar," said Morgan. "I bet we just have to get our stuff there and set things up. My grandma does the bazaar every year and she usually just works a few hours, not all day."

"So, it's set?" asked Chelsea. "Five elves for Daddy's float?"

"Does he pay?" asked Amy.

Chelsea laughed. "Are you kidding? My dad thinks we should all be honored just to ride on his precious float. But I can probably talk him into lunch afterward."

"It's a date," said Carlie.

So it was settled. The five girls would play Santa's elves in the parade and then work like elves the rest of the time.

Morgan just hoped that there would be enough time to do everything. She knew that it wasn't up to her to make sure that this all worked out, but she couldn't help but feel somewhat responsible. Mostly she didn't want to see any of the girls lose money on the ski trip. Well, besides Chelsea … and only because she could afford it.

The rain had almost completely stopped by the time the group started to break up. Amy had to leave early to help at her parents' restaurant. Chelsea had to go because her mom was picking her up, and Carlie had to get home to help her mom watch the boys. Then it was just Emily and Morgan.

"Did you mind what I said?" asked Emily as they were putting on their raincoats.

"About what?"

"You know … about all of us going on the ski trip. I saw you giving me the evil eye."

"I guess I was just surprised. I was ready to give it up and just forget it."

"After your big speech about faith?"

"I just wasn't sure whether I was having faith in God or faith in Morgan."

Emily laughed. "Maybe it was both."

"I just hope it works out."

"Sure, it will," said Emily. "We'll be praying about it, won't we?"

"Of course." Morgan glanced at Emily. "What made you change your mind like that? I mean, this morning you seemed so sure that you couldn't make enough money to go ... and now you're all cool with it."

"I got to thinking about Cory and Janna ..."

"Huh?"

"I was just thinking about how much I've learned in youth group these past several months ... and I thought maybe Amy, Chelsea, and Carlie would like to be around them for a while too. I mean, not to recruit them into our church or anything ..."

"I get it," said Morgan as she locked the bus door.

"Is that weird?"

Morgan shook her head. "No, that is very cool." She smiled at Emily. "I think your faith is bigger than mine."

"No way," said Emily.

"Way."

"Hey, I asked my mom about going to your house for Thanksgiving ... and you know what she told me?"

"No."

"She said she'd love to come, except that she already invited Mr. Greeley to come to our house for Thanksgiving."

"Really?" Morgan tried to imagine old Mr. Greeley sitting at the kitchen table with Emily, her mom, and her sixteen-year-old brother, Kyle.

"Pretty weird, huh?"

"No … I mean Mr. Greeley is a nice old guy. And I know he really likes you and your family, Em."

"Still, it'll be sort of odd … I mean he's not exactly talkative. And Kyle is still kind of afraid of him."

"That's just because he doesn't know him." Morgan remembered how she used to be afraid of strange Mr. Greeley too — back before he gave them the keys to their clubhouse. "I know!" said Morgan suddenly. "Why don't you guys just bring Mr. Greeley over to our house for Thanksgiving? You know, the more the merrier."

"That sounds good to me. I'll check with Mom and get back to you."

"Hopefully, you guys can come. I have it all planned out," said Morgan. "I should have figured out the socks by then, and you and I can get a head start by cutting out a bunch of them."

"And can I sew them too?"

"Sure," said Morgan. "You were doing really good on my sewing machine when we made the pillows and stuff for the bus."

"Cool." Emily gave her a high five. "And I'm so excited about the ski trip. It's going to be awesome!"

Morgan hugged Emily. "I'm so glad you changed your mind about the ski trip," she said happily. "I guess my faith was starting to shrink. I think I would've given up on the trip if you hadn't said something just when you did."

Emily grinned. "Guess that's what friends are for, huh?"

Morgan thought about that as she walked home. It was hard to remember what life had been like before Emily moved here last spring. It seemed like they'd been friends forever, but in reality it had only been about six months, give or take. Still, Morgan knew that theirs was a friendship that would last forever. And if for some reason Emily was unable to go on the ski trip, Morgan would gladly forfeit her spot as well. She wouldn't care if it was completely paid for, or if all the other girls were going. Morgan would stay home with Emily.

She just hoped it wouldn't come down to that. And she'd be praying extra hard to make sure that it didn't!

chapter three

"I'm so bummed," said Carlie as the four friends walked to school on Monday.

"What's up?" asked Amy.

"Chelsea called me last night — I couldn't believe it — she invited me to go with her and her family to the ski resort."

"Wow," said Emily. "That sounds awesome."

"Yeah," agreed Morgan, "Why are you bummed about that?"

Carlie kicked a stone off the sidewalk. "Because my parents said 'no way, José.'"

"Why?" asked Emily.

"Because it's Thanksgiving," said Carlie. "My parents are so old-fashioned. They think the world will come to an end if all of our family — I mean aunts and uncles and cousins and everyone — isn't together under one roof for that entire day."

"That's kind of nice," said Morgan. "I can't imagine having that much family around."

Carlie let out a long sigh. "Yeah, there's like eighty people. They all come to my aunt's house, which usually seems pretty roomy, but it's so crowded in there you can hardly breathe.

And noisy? Have you ever been to a Latino celebration? Man, your ears are ringing for three days afterward."

The girls laughed.

"Well, my parents are old-fashioned too," said Amy. "But not about holidays. For my parents, the holidays are just a time to make money in the restaurant. I'll be working on Thanksgiving."

"Really?" asked Emily. "Do very many people eat Chinese food on Thanksgiving?"

"You'd be surprised," said Amy. "I think most of our holiday customers don't have family around. But at least they're generous with their tips. Even so, I'd give anything to have Carlie's problem. I wish Chelsea would invite me to go skiing with her."

"Maybe she will," said Carlie sadly.

They were almost at Boscoe Bay Middle School now.

"Well, cheer up," said Emily, "At least you have the ski trip after Christmas to look forward to."

"Yeah," said Carlie. "After my parents nixed my chances of going with Chelsea, I asked about the ski trip, and it sounded like it might be okay. My mom even agreed to pay me to watch the boys while she gets ready for Christmas, and my dad offered to help us to go cut down Christmas trees to sell at the bazaar."

"That's great," said Morgan. "Maybe that whole thing with Chelsea helped to soften them up."

Carlie laughed. "Yeah, that's what I was thinking too."

"Speaking of Chelsea," said Amy, pointing to the Mercedes that was just pulling up in front of the school. "There she is."

"Hey, Chelsea," called Carlie, waving.

Chelsea came over to join them as they went up the steps to the front entrance. "I'm still mad at you," Chelsea said to Carlie with a pouting face.

Carlie shrugged. "Hey, I can't help what my parents say."

"At least we still have the ski trip to look forward to after Christmas," Morgan reminded her. "I'm going to pick up the forms today."

"I already have my deposit money," said Amy. "It's at home, but I counted it out last night and I have just enough."

"And my dad will give me a check for the whole thing," said Chelsea.

"And I was just telling these guys that my parents said I can go to that — since it's not actually on Christmas," said Carlie as they went inside the school. "My mom even offered to advance me some babysitting money so I can pay the deposit."

Emily glanced at Morgan with an uneasy expression as they walked to their lockers. Morgan could tell that she was still a little worried about the money. But Morgan smiled at her in a way she hoped was reassuring.

"It's going to be so cool," Morgan said to her friends. "All five of us up there, skiing and riding and having a totally great time."

"I think I want to try snowboarding," said Carlie.

"Yeah, and I should be pretty good at it by then," added Chelsea.

"I'm going to ski," said Amy. "I think it looks more graceful."

"Snowboarding's more fun," said Emily.

"How do *you* know?" Amy asked her.

"Because I've done it."

Morgan blinked. "You've gone snowboarding before, Emily?"

"Yeah, when we lived in Idaho." Emily got a worried look now, and Morgan knew that it was because she didn't like to mention where they'd moved from. "I mean when we were in Idaho ... we went a few times."

"Have you been to Sun Valley?" asked Chelsea.

"No," said Emily. "Not to ride anyway. We went there once just to check it out."

"My sister has been there. She says it's awesome."

Just then the warning bell rang, and the girls scattered off toward their first-period classes. But as Morgan and Emily went to English, Morgan had to ask. "You've really been snowboarding before?"

"Yeah, I thought I told you."

"No." Morgan shook her head. "Are you any good?"

Emily shrugged. "Not the first time … but I kinda got the hang of it. It's not that hard, really. And you're pretty athletic, Morgan, so you shouldn't have any problem. Have you ever skateboarded?"

"No."

"Oh." Emily grinned. "My brother taught me to skateboard when I was like six. I could probably borrow Kyle's board and give you some lessons. It's all about balance."

"All right," said Morgan as they took their seats. Then as Mrs. Robertson began to drone on about punctuation and sentence structure, Morgan began to daydream about snowboarding down a white snowy peak. Naturally, she was able to do this with grace and style. And, Morgan realized, in her daydream her hair was loose and flowing. Maybe it was time to lose the beaded braids. Morgan fingered a braid. Her hair was past her shoulders now. She wondered what it would look like without the braids. Perhaps she could get the curl relaxed a little, the way her mother did.

"Morgan Evans?" A shrill voice interrupted her daydreaming.

Morgan adjusted her glasses and looked up at Mrs. Robertson who was looking directly at Morgan.

"Can you tell me ... does this sentence require a semicolon or a comma?"

Morgan studied the sentence that Mrs. Robertson was pointing to on the board. She had no idea which was the right answer, but since there was a fifty-fifty chance, she decided to guess. "A comma."

"No," said Mrs. Robertson crisply. "And if you had been listening, you would've known that this particular sentence requires a semicolon," and then she went on to explain the reason why. Although, even as Morgan listened, she wasn't so sure she got it. Why wouldn't a comma work just as well? Just the same, this little embarrassment was a good reminder that she needed to pay attention. Daydreaming was okay when you weren't at school, but Morgan knew that it would be a mistake to get behind in class.

At noon, Morgan went to their regular table in the cafeteria. As usual, Morgan had a sack lunch from home. And, as usual, she and Carlie and Amy were the first ones at their table. This was because the three of them usually brought lunches from home. Morgan felt like they were the lucky ones. Amy mostly brought food from the restaurant. Carlie usually had something that smelled delightfully Mexican. And Morgan had whatever Grandma had decided she needed for that day. Morgan knew that Emily ate the cafeteria food for two reasons. One reason was top secret: because

Emily was entitled to vouchers. Fortunately, their school's vouchers looked exactly like regular lunch tickets. The other reason was because Emily's mother wasn't much into cooking. The reason Chelsea ate cafeteria food was a mystery. But Chelsea claimed she liked it. For the most part, Chelsea ate the same thing everyday — salad and diet soda. Morgan didn't think it was the most healthy or even appetizing meal, but she had learned early on that it was better not to mention this to Chelsea.

"You are not going to believe this," said Emily as she and Chelsea sat down to join them.

"What?" asked Morgan.

"Chelsea invited *me* to go to the resort with her and her family."

"No way," said Amy with a disappointed frown. "Why didn't you ask me, Chelsea?"

Chelsea shrugged. "I thought you had to work, Amy."

"I would've gotten out of it." Amy scowled. "I suppose this means that only Morgan, Carlie, and I will be going to Miss McPhearson's tea now."

"Sorry to miss that," said Emily. "Tell her hello for me, okay?"

"But why Emily?" demanded Amy, still unwilling to give it up. "You guys aren't even that good of friends."

"For one thing, Emily actually knows how to snowboard." Chelsea stuck a straw in her soda. "So she was kinda ahead of the game after Carlie dropped out."

"I am so jealous," said Carlie.

"I'm sorry," said Emily. "If you could've gone I wouldn't —"

"That's okay," said Carlie. She smiled at Chelsea now. "I'm glad you have someone to go with you."

Chelsea nodded. "Yeah, that'll make it more fun."

Morgan just stared at Emily. Was she honestly planning on going with Chelsea? Those two didn't even get along that well. "How do you even know you can go yet, Emily?" she asked as she opened a plastic bag and removed half a sandwich.

"I let her use my phone," said Chelsea. "She already called her mom at work."

"And Mom said it was fine."

Morgan wanted to ask her what this meant about Thanksgiving. Were Emily's mom and brother and Mr. Greeley still coming to Morgan's house? But she couldn't think of a way to say it without sounding mad. Instead, she just focused on her lunch. Meanwhile, the other girls chattered away about snowboarding and clothes and most of it went right over Morgan's head.

By the end of the day, Morgan knew that she was jealous. But she also knew that she didn't want anyone to know. As usual, the five girls met at their lockers.

"It's weird not having soccer to go to," said Chelsea as she closed her locker.

"And basketball doesn't start up until after Christmas," said Carlie.

"Well, I'm going to go by the church and pick up the forms for the ski trip," said Morgan. "If anyone wants to get one, they'll be at the clubhouse."

"Do you need a ride?" asked Chelsea. "My mom's picking me up."

Morgan considered this. On one hand she felt sort of mad at Chelsea right now ... but on the other hand, it was a quite a walk to the other end of town to get to the church and then all the way back home again. "Sure," she told Chelsea. "That'd be nice."

"Anyone else?" offered Chelsea.

"I have to go to the restaurant," said Amy. "Work, work, work ... all I do is work."

Emily laughed. "Yeah, right. I've seen how busy it is at the restaurant this time of day. You and your sisters and brother usually watch TV and eat."

Amy made a face, then laughed. "Well, I can complain if I want to."

"And I have to get home to watch my brothers," said Carlie. "Mom and Tia Maria are getting a head start on Thanksgiving shopping. But at least I'll be earning money for the ski trip."

Then Carlie and Amy left to walk home together.

"How about you, Emily?" asked Chelsea. "Want a ride?"

"Sounds good."

So the three of them went out to wait for Chelsea's mom. As they waited, Chelsea and Emily discussed what Emily would need to bring on Thursday. Morgan pretended to be distracted with a sketch she was creating on the front of her notebook. It was a tiger, partially hidden behind a tree.

"You can borrow my old ski pants," said Chelsea. "In fact, you can have them. I don't need them anymore."

"Cool," said Emily. "What color are they?"

"They're just navy blue, but they are Tommy Hilfiger," said Chelsea. "In fact, you can have the jacket that goes with them too. It's a little tight on me anyway, and I don't think you're as big on top as I am."

"Bragging again, are you?" teased Emily.

Chelsea laughed. *"We all develop at different rates,"* she said in a voice that Morgan knew was an imitation of their health teacher, Miss Perrell.

"Yes," said Emily in the same tone. *"And we do not make fun of others just because their bodies are different than ours."*

"There's my mom," said Chelsea.

Soon all three were in Chelsea's car. "I told Morgan we'd give her a lift to her church so she can get the stuff for the ski trip."

"That's fine," said Mrs. Landers. "Hello, Emily and Morgan. I haven't seen you two since the park project. How's it going?"

"Okay," said Morgan in a slightly flat tone.

"Good," said Emily. "Thanks."

"Guess what, Mom?"

"What?"

"Emily is going to come with us to the resort for Thanksgiving."

"That's wonderful. I was just feeling sad that you wouldn't have a friend up there. Meredith and Jason are each bringing someone." She glanced at Emily. "Are your parents okay with that? Do I need to call them or anything?"

"She just has a mom," said Chelsea in a quiet voice.

"Yes, that's right. I knew that. Is your mother all right with you going?"

"Yeah," said Emily. "Chelsea let me call my mom on her cell phone. And it's okay. I mean, as long as Mom knows where we'll be and phone numbers and all that sort of thing."

"I'll write it all out," said Mrs. Landers. "Chelsea can bring it to school tomorrow. And your mom can call me if she has any questions."

Morgan kept her eyes on her drawing of the tiger. But as she filled in the stripes, she felt seriously jealous and angry. Plus, she kept asking herself, why hadn't she simply walked to the church? The exercise probably would've helped with her attitude — and she wouldn't have been subjected to all this.

"You can just drop me off at the church, Mrs. Landers," said Morgan in voice that sounded much brighter than she felt. Still, she thought this might be a way to escape the little happy party going on between Chelsea and Emily right now.

"Don't you want a ride back home?" asked Chelsea.

"No, I need to talk to Pastor George about something," Morgan told them, although that wasn't completely true. But she would make it true. She would go and tell Pastor George about her jealousy fit, and perhaps he would straighten her out. It seemed like a good plan. "I can just walk home afterward."

"Well, if you're sure," said Mrs. Landers as she pulled up in front of the church.

"Yes," said Morgan. "And the exercise will do me good."

"But while we're here," said Mrs. Landers, "Why don't I just make out a check for the ski trip. Then it will be all taken care of."

"Works for me," said Chelsea. "I'll go in with Morgan and get the form while you write the check."

"I'll go in too," said Emily.

So the three of them went into the church office together, where Chelsea and Emily each picked up their own forms and Morgan got three.

"I'm going to take this out to my mom to fill out," said Chelsea after Morgan introduced her to the church secretary.

"At this rate, it looks like you're going to fill up the whole ski trip, Morgan," said Mrs. Albert. "Cory and Janna should be pleased."

Morgan folded the papers and slipped them into her backpack. "I don't think I can fill up the whole ski trip, Mrs. Albert. Just five spots ... for me and my friends."

"Well, good for you." Mrs. Albert smiled. "And you're going too, Emily?"

"I hope so," said Emily.

Morgan was about to ask if Pastor George was around, but then realized that it could pose a problem to her escape plan if he wasn't there right now. So she decided to just chat with Mrs. Albert. "We're going to be making things for the bazaar," she said. "And our friend Carlie's dad is going to help us cut down Christmas trees, and we'll make wreaths and things to sell so that we can earn our way for the ski trip."

"Sounds like you girls have a busy month ahead."

Just then Chelsea reappeared with her completed form and check. "Here you go," she told Mrs. Albert. "All set."

"Well, we've had a few deposits, but you're the first one to be paid in full, Chelsea. Thank you."

"No problem," said Chelsea. "Ready to roll, Em?"

"See ya later, Morgan," called Emily.

"Yeah," said Chelsea. "Later."

Then Morgan was alone in the office with Mrs. Albert. She felt embarrassed and slightly abandoned, and wasn't even sure that she really wanted to talk to Pastor George now.

"Was there something else you needed, dear?" asked Mrs. Albert.

"No," said Morgan. She felt a lump growing in her throat.

"Why didn't you leave with your friends?"

"I ... uh ... I wanted to walk home," she said, blinking back tears.

"Oh ..."

Then Morgan said good-bye and turned and slowly made her way to the front door. She wanted to be sure that the Mercedes was completely out of sight. It was. So she went out and began walking back toward home. Alone. The lump in her throat was growing bigger, and the breeze off the ocean was picking up. And, before long, the wind began to chill the tears that had sneaked down her cheeks.

chapter four

"Are you mad at me?" Emily asked Morgan on Wednesday.

"No, of course not," said Morgan. The two of them were in the clubhouse, getting ready for the others to arrive for a quick Thanksgiving party that Amy had insisted they needed to have. Although Amy, at the moment, was nowhere to be seen.

"But you've been acting different," said Emily.

"Different than what?" asked Morgan as she set out napkins and paper cups.

"Different like you're mad or something."

Morgan turned to face Emily now. Maybe it was time to be honest. "I guess I'm hurt," she said.

"Because I'm going with Chelsea?"

Morgan shrugged. "I'd been looking forward to you coming over for Thanksgiving … I thought we were going to work on the polar socks."

"But we can do that next week," said Emily.

"I know, but …"

Just then Amy walked in carrying a pink box. "Happy Thanksgiving," she said as she set the box on the table. "I made these myself."

"Ooh, those are pretty," said Emily as Amy opened the box to display cupcakes frosted in shades of yellow, orange, and gold and topped with candy corn.

"Chocolate," said Amy. "And see how I tinted the frosting different colors?"

"These are really nice," said Morgan.

"Here come Chelsea and Carlie," said Emily, pointing out the window.

"Happy Thanksgiving," said Chelsea as she set down a grocery bag. "I brought chips and soda."

"I'll put some music on," offered Emily, going over to the old-fashioned record player and selecting a vinyl record.

Soon the five of them were eating and laughing and talking, and Morgan began to feel a little bit better, telling herself that it was just like old times. She knew she shouldn't be so bummed about the fact that Emily was going to do something with Chelsea. All five of them were friends. And it was okay to do things with different people. Maybe she'd invite Carlie and Amy over during the weekend to work on socks. Morgan knew that jealousy was a sin. And she was going to do everything she could to get over it.

"The elf costumes for the Christmas parade arrived," said Chelsea. "And I hate to admit it, but they're pretty geeky looking." She made a face. "I thought maybe we could rework them somehow since we don't want to look like freaks up there on the float." She pointed at Morgan. "You're pretty good at that sort of thing. Maybe you can think of a way to make them look cool."

"Sure," said Morgan.

"Let's plan on getting together next week then." Chelsea looked at her watch and then at Emily. "Uh-oh, Em, we gotta go. My mom is probably already at your house by now."

"But it's not even five," said Morgan.

"I know. We're supposed to be on the road at five," said Chelsea. "They have this big dinner at the lodge tonight, with live music and everything. We don't wanna be late."

"Sorry we can't stay to clean up," said Emily as Chelsea tugged her by the arm. "You guys have a good Thanksgiving."

"You too," called Amy.

"Don't break any bones," added Carlie.

"Have fun," said Morgan, although her heart was not in it.

"I have to go too," said Amy. "The restaurant is calling …"

"Me too," said Carlie. "I told Mom I'd watch the boys tonight while she's making Mexican wedding cakes."

"Who's getting married?" asked Amy as she pulled on her parka.

"No one," said Carlie. "They're actually just cookies, but Mom likes to make them for holidays."

"I'll clean up," said Morgan as she picked up the paper plates and napkins and tossed them into a bag.

"Thanks!" called Carlie and Amy in unison. "See ya."

Morgan took her time cleaning up the bus. She put all the garbage away, then put the leftover sodas in the fridge and the chips in the cupboard. She wiped down the table and the counter and sink. Then she even went around and fluffed the pillows and things before she finally unplugged the strings of lights and turned off the heater. "Good-bye, old faithful bus," she said as she turned off the last light. "Happy Thanksgiving."

Back at her house, Morgan retreated to her bedroom. She knew that her mom was going out tonight with some single girlfriends who got together occasionally. She also knew that since it was Wednesday, Grandma would expect her to go to midweek service with her. The problem was that Morgan did not feel like going. She knew she should probably go anyway. Pastor George often said that the best time to go to church was when you felt the least like going, but somehow she didn't think she could force herself tonight.

Morgan's plan was to lie low. She would keep the light off in her room and pretend to be napping. Maybe Grandma would lose track of the time and forget all about going to church. After all, she was pretty wrapped up with getting things ready for tomorrow's Thanksgiving feast. Because, as it turned out, Emily's family and Mr. Greeley were still coming over. Just another reminder for Morgan that her best friend was off having fun with someone else.

At quarter past seven, it was late enough that Morgan knew they wouldn't be going to church. But now she felt a little concerned too — as well as hungry. Grandma would usually have called Morgan to dinner by now. Maybe she actually went to church without her. Morgan went out into the living room and looked around. No Grandma. The kitchen was dark too. Then Morgan checked out the kitchen window, peeking into the carport, but Grandma's car was there. Was it possible that Grandma had gone out with someone else tonight? Morgan looked around to see if there was a note. No note.

Finally Morgan decided to peek into Grandma's room, although it seemed unlikely that she'd be in here. And there, with only a bedside lamp on, Grandma was stretched out on top of her bed with her Bible still open in her lap. Morgan felt a jolt of panic, like something was seriously wrong — was Grandma dead? Then she walked closer and saw that Grandma was breathing. She was simply asleep. Morgan tiptoed out of the bedroom and went to the kitchen to find something to eat. It looked like Grandma had been busy today. Lots of things, including several yummy-looking pies, were all ready to go for tomorrow. A big turkey occupied most of the refrigerator. No wonder Grandma was so tired.

Morgan fixed herself a peanut butter sandwich and a glass of milk, which she took to the living room to eat in front of the

TV. Normally, this wasn't allowed, but since Mom was gone and Grandma was asleep, who would know? She turned on the TV, going to the Disney channel, but the show playing, of course, was about a ski trip. Morgan turned off the TV and ate her sandwich in silence. All she could think was that, right now, Emily was with Chelsea, having the time of her life. She was enjoying a fancy dinner in a ski lodge, complete with live music — how could Morgan ever compete with something like that?

"What are you doing, Morgan?" asked Grandma as she came out of her bedroom.

"Oh …" Morgan looked up with a guilty expression. "I was all alone and hungry … and I just thought —"

"I'm sorry," said Grandma as she looked at the clock on the wall. "I had no idea it was so late. I thought I'd take a little rest. Goodness, what happened to the time?"

"It looks like you were busy today," said Morgan as she polished off the last of her milk. "Sorry I wasn't around to help."

"Oh, that's all right."

Morgan followed Grandma into the kitchen. But it seemed like Grandma was moving slower than usual. "Are you okay?" Morgan asked her.

Grandma turned and looked at her. "Well, yes … just tired, I guess …" She smiled. "Getting old."

"Anything I can help you with?" offered Morgan.

"Not tonight ... but I might take you up on that tomorrow. Did you get enough to eat, dear?"

"Yeah, I'm fine." Then Morgan sat on the kitchen stool and watched as Grandma put a bowl of soup into the microwave.

"Are you still feeling badly about Emily not being here for Thanksgiving?"

Morgan shrugged. "I'm okay." She'd already confessed some of her sadness to Grandma, but now she wanted to pretend like it wasn't such a big deal.

"Have you tried out the sock pattern with the tiger stripes yet?" Grandma sat down on the stool opposite Morgan and dipped her spoon into the soup she'd just heated. "I found some other nice remnants of polar fleece the other day. I think there might be enough for several pairs of socks."

"I haven't tried the pattern yet," admitted Morgan. "I'd been hoping that Emily and I could work on it tomorrow and into the weekend ... but that's not going to happen."

"Maybe you and I could work on it together," offered Grandma.

"Sure," said Morgan. And she knew it was nice of Grandma to want to help and she didn't want to hurt her feelings, but it just wouldn't be the same as having Emily here.

The next morning, Morgan did what she could to help Grandma in the kitchen. But with Mom home, it seemed more like Morgan was in the way. And then when Mr. Greeley and

Emily's family came, all Morgan could think was that it wasn't fair that Emily wasn't here. She tried to be polite during dinner, but all she wanted to do was to get away from these people. It was all wrong. Finally, as everyone was taking a break before dessert, Morgan excused herself.

"I think I'll take a walk," she said.

"Right now?" said Mom with a creased brow. "It's raining like the dickens out there."

"I'll wear my rain slicker." And then Morgan made a quick exit. But Mom was right; it was really coming down hard. Soon Morgan found herself unlocking the door to the clubhouse. She turned on the heater and the string of lights and proceeded to make herself at home. She tried not to think about what Emily and Chelsea were doing right now. But it was like telling herself not to think about pink elephants — the more she tried to push it from her mind, the more obsessed she became. Since it was raining down here, it was probably snowing up there. Snow sure seemed a lot nicer than rain. She wondered if Emily was wearing Chelsea's Tommy Hilfiger outfit. Were they having a great time riding down the mountain together? Was Emily as good as Chelsea? Or maybe she was better. Morgan remembered Emily's promise to give Morgan lessons on Kyle's skateboard, but that hadn't happened yet. Finally, Morgan was sick and tired of thinking about Emily and Chelsea. Maybe being stuck at home with her family and Emily's and even Mr. Greeley would be better than this!

Besides, Morgan told herself as she jogged back through the rain, she could start making polar socks. If she set her mind to it, she might even have several pairs finished by the end of the day. She wondered how many pairs it would take to make fifty dollars — five pairs if she charged ten for each pair, but that seemed a little steep.

"You're back," said Mom as Morgan burst in out of the rain.

"Yeah, it's pretty wet out there."

"Well, Mr. Greeley and Lisa and Kyle just left."

"Did they already have dessert?"

"Yes, and everyone was starting to act sleepy. I think they all went home to take a nap."

"That sounds good to me," said Grandma.

"Yes," said Mom. "You go and have a rest. Morgan and I will clean up in here."

Morgan wanted to protest this idea, but knew that would be selfish … especially since she hadn't helped much to get things ready. So she rolled up her sleeves and helped Mom to put the kitchen back in order.

"Grandma said that you were missing Emily," said Mom as she handed Morgan a pan to dry.

Morgan just shrugged. "I guess …"

"Lisa said that Emily had been so thrilled to go, Morgan. You know life hasn't been exactly easy for them this past year. Emily has been through a lot. Really, you should be happy for her."

Morgan forced a smile. "Okay, I am happy for her. I guess I'm just sad for me."

Mom laughed and gave Morgan a little hug. "Well, at least that's honest."

"And I'm worried," confessed Morgan.

"About what?"

"Well, what if Emily and Chelsea become best friends?"

"I suppose that could happen ..." Mom handed Morgan a pie tin to dry. "At least you have several good friends, Morgan. There's Carlie and Amy still."

"I know ... but Emily is my best friend."

"Then my guess is that she will continue to be your best friend."

"I hope so."

"Morgan ..." Mom had a slightly worried expression now.

"What?"

"Well, I'm concerned about your grandma."

"Why?"

"She hasn't been feeling well lately. She's very tired and ... and it seems like she's just not herself."

"What's wrong?"

"I don't know. I'm encouraging her to see the doctor, but she thinks it's just old age."

"How old is Grandma anyway?"

"Not that old. She's not even seventy yet."

"Oh." Morgan didn't want to admit it, but that seemed pretty old.

"Anyway, until we can get her to go to the doctor, I want both of us to help out more around here. Are you okay with that?"

"Of course."

"Maybe we can take turns fixing dinner," said Mom.

Morgan made a face. "But we're not as good at cooking as Grandma."

"I know. But that might be because we never get the chance to practice."

"But Grandma loves to cook."

"Well, we can help with other things too. You're old enough to do your own laundry. And I can start doing some of the grocery shopping."

Morgan studied Mom for a moment. "Do you really think she's sick?"

Mom just shook her head. "I don't know."

So when Morgan went to bed on Thanksgiving night, she had two things to worry about — losing her best friend, and her grandmother's health. But instead of worrying, Morgan did something better. She prayed.

chapter five

When Morgan got up on the day after Thanksgiving, she discovered Grandma sitting at the kitchen table with her sewing basket and a small pile of colorful polar fleece. "Good morning," said Grandma brightly.

"Good morning." Morgan eyed the fleece. "Is that for making socks?"

"Yes. I thought you and I could work on it together. Your mom already went to open up her shop early. You know what they say about today."

"Black Friday?" asked Morgan.

Grandma chuckled. "Yes, the biggest shopping day of the year."

"I wish I had thought about that sooner," said Morgan. "I could've had some socks all made up to sell in Mom's shop today."

"Oh, well," said Grandma. "No use crying over spilt milk."

"Did you have breakfast already?" asked Morgan.

Grandma smiled sheepishly. "Well, I wasn't very hungry after all that feasting yesterday. I had pumpkin pie and coffee. Are you hungry?" Grandma started to get up.

"No," said Morgan quickly. "I just want cold cereal. I can get it."

Grandma held up the paper pattern. "I've been reading the instructions. I see that we use this pattern as a model to create several other patterns in various sizes."

"Oh, yeah," said Morgan as she filled a bowl with Cheerios. "I never even thought about sizes."

"Apparently somebody else did. While you're up, do you want to get me that roll of butcher paper out of the drawer?"

Morgan found the paper and handed it to Grandma, then sat down across from her and began eating cereal.

"I'll just trace these out on the paper," said Grandma as she adjusted her glasses. "You can cut them."

By noon they had all the patterns cut, and Morgan was just getting ready to cut out the fabric when Grandma seemed to grow weary. "Why don't you go have a rest," said Morgan. "I can work on these."

"I do feel tired," said Grandma.

Morgan stood up now. "Come on," she urged as she helped Grandma up. "You have a little nap and then you can help me later, okay?"

"You and Cleo," said Grandma. "You're treating me like an old lady."

"Because we love you," said Morgan.

Grandma laughed as she walked, but Morgan also noticed that she put her hand on the counter to balance herself. That was not like her.

"Come on, Grandma," said Morgan as she took her by the arm. "Let me walk with you."

"I do feel a little unsteady sometimes," admitted Grandma. "A little light-headed when I stand up."

"Mom said you need to go to the doctor," said Morgan as she walked her to her bedroom.

"Oh, I don't know about —"

"And while you're resting, I'm going to call Dr. Ballister and make an appointment for you."

"Oh, you are, are you?" Grandma peered at Morgan.

"Isn't that what you would do for me if I was feeling sick?"

Grandma chuckled as Morgan helped her to her bed. "You're growing up too fast, Morgan. It seems like only yesterday that I was putting you down for a nap ... now you're doing the same to me."

Morgan laid Grandma's crocheted afghan over her legs. "Just rest, Grandma. I'll see if I can get you an appointment for next week. Okay?"

"Whatever you say, dear."

So Morgan closed the door behind her and went out and looked up Dr. Ballister's phone number. She explained the concerns they had about Grandma as well as the symptoms of tiredness and dizziness and the nurse made an appointment for the following Tuesday. Morgan wrote down the time and date, thanked her, and hung up.

Morgan returned to the kitchen, and instead of going back to her sewing project, she cleaned up the breakfast dishes, washed out the coffee pot, and then went back to cutting out socks. She realized right away that it would be important to pin the pieces together so that the sizes didn't get mixed up. She also made some mistakes with cutting the fabric with the wrong side out. But finally, she had what appeared to be eight pairs of socks, in various sizes, ready to sew together. It really didn't seem too complicated.

"How's it going?" asked Grandma as Morgan was setting up her sewing machine.

"You're up from your nap," said Morgan. "Feeling better?"

"I can hardly believe I slept so long. Do you know that it's after one already?"

Morgan showed her how many pairs of socks she cut out. "I was just about to sew up this first pair. They're my size, so I thought I could test them out to make sure I'm doing it right."

"Good thinking. And don't forget to use the knit stitch. It takes longer, but it's the only way you can sew a stretchy fabric like that fleece without having the seams pop open."

"I know," said Morgan. "I just wish it wasn't such a slow way to sew."

"Better slowly than holey."

Morgan laughed as she changed the stitch setting. "Some people might like 'holy' socks."

"Not ones with holes in them. And while you're doing that, I'll go put us together some lunch. We have some fine-looking turkey leftovers."

"Sounds yummy."

By the time Grandma called her to lunch, Morgan had one sock completely finished in the tiger design. She proudly took it in to show Grandma.

"It looks fine, Morgan. Did it fit okay?"

"I haven't tried it yet." Morgan sat down in a chair in the living room and peeled off her shoe and sock. "I guess it doesn't matter which foot I put it on, does it?"

"Not for socks, dear."

"Ugh," groaned Morgan as she tried to force her foot into the sock. "This is not working … not at all."

"Let me see," said Grandma.

Morgan handed her the sock. "It doesn't stretch, you know, to go over my foot. It's too tight."

Grandma examined the sock and finally nodded. "I see what's wrong."

"What?"

Grandma stretched the fabric. "See?"

"What?"

"The stretch is going the wrong way. You need to cut them out so that the stretch goes widthwise. This one goes lengthwise. That's why you couldn't get your foot into it."

"Oh no," said Morgan. "I never thought about that when I cut out the other socks. What if they're all wrong?"

"I doubt that they'll all be wrong, dear."

"But some of them will be."

"At least it was only remnant fabric," said Grandma. "Come and have some lunch, and we'll figure it out later."

"I can't believe I was so stupid," said Morgan as she sat down at the kitchen table. "You've told me about the grain of the fabric before."

After lunch, they went to Morgan's room to see what could be done about the sock dilemma. Morgan held up a pair of cut-out socks that were neatly pinned together. "I thought I was being so careful," she said, "and all I did was mess things up."

"Don't be so hard on yourself. I probably would've done the same thing. I've knit socks before, but making them out of fabric is new to me too." Grandma sat on Morgan's bed and examined the pieces that she had cut out, separating into two piles the ones that were going the right way from the ones that were going the wrong way. But the wrong-way pile was getting bigger and bigger.

"This is hopeless," said Morgan as she flopped down into her beanbag chair.

Grandma chuckled. "Well, it looks like you have two pairs that are cut in the right direction."

"All that work for just two pairs of socks," said Morgan sadly. "And I haven't even sewn them yet."

"Just consider it a learning experience."

"But what about all the fabric I wasted?" Morgan looked at the big pile of colorful pieces.

Grandma smiled. "Well, don't throw these away. I think I might be able to piece them together for a quilt."

"A sock quilt?"

Grandma laughed. "Maybe so … maybe so …"

"I guess I should be glad that Emily isn't here."

"Why's that, dear?"

"Because she'd probably think I was an idiot to waste all this time and fabric to produce just two pairs of socks."

"You haven't even produced those yet," Grandma reminded her. "Why don't you sew them up and see how it goes. Then maybe we can make a trip to the fabric store and get some more polar fleece fabric. They're having a big sale today."

"You want to go shopping on Black Friday?"

Grandma patted her on the head. "If it'll help get you out of these doldrums, I do." Then she winked at Morgan. "Besides, you know me, I'm always happy to go to the fabric store."

So Morgan sewed up the socks and was surprised that it didn't take as long as she thought it would. She even tried a pair on — the ones with red and white stripes — and they fit perfectly. She proudly modeled them for Grandma.

"How do they feel?"

"Great. I think I'll keep them." Then Morgan looked at the other pair. They were soft pastel colors. "Hey, these are your size, Grandma. Why don't you try them on?"

"Oh, I don't want to —"

"Come on," said Morgan. "Just try them."

So Grandma slipped off her slippers and pulled on the fuzzy socks. "Very nice," she said, pointing a toe.

"They're for you," proclaimed Morgan.

"Thank you very much."

Then Grandma and Morgan went to the fabric store. Morgan only had twelve dollars of her own money, but Grandma offered to help out. "Look at all these colors," said Morgan as they walked down the aisle of polar fleece fabric. "I don't know how I'll decide." But before long, Morgan had picked out a stack of bolts. Grandma helped her to figure out the yardage, and according to their estimates, Morgan would be able to make about thirty pairs of socks when she was all done. "That's if I don't cut them wrong," said Morgan as they went out to the car.

"I think today's lesson will take care of that."

"Thanks for your help, Grandma," said Morgan as she opened the bag and fingered the soft fabric. "Do you think eight dollars a pair is too much?"

"I think that sounds about right for handmade socks," said Grandma. "I know my feet are nice and cozy right now. And these socks are just perfect for my rain boots."

By Saturday afternoon, Morgan had sewn up three pairs of socks. She was just about to start another pair when Grandma called her to come out of her room. "Amy is here to see you," she said.

"Oh, hi, Amy," said Morgan, wondering why Amy had on a dress. "What's up?"

"Miss McPhearson's tea," said Amy in a slightly irritated tone. "And you do not look ready to go."

Morgan slapped her forehead. "Oh, man, I totally forgot." She looked at the clock on the wall. "Do I have time to change real quick?"

"Just hurry," commanded Amy. "Carlie is in the car. My sister An is driving us over there."

Morgan rushed back to her room, opened her closet, and pulled out a dark green velvet jumper that Grandma made for her last Christmas. She didn't really like the jumper because she felt it looked too juvenile. But she figured Miss McPhearson might appreciate it. And it would make Grandma happy. Hopefully it wasn't too small. She tugged it over her white turtleneck, and fortunately it fit. Then she shoved her feet into her black knee-high boots and added a beaded necklace. She grabbed up her coat and was about to hurry out when she noticed a finished pair of purple socks on her bed. Would it be too weird to give them to Miss McPhearson? She stuffed them into her coat pocket, and then hurried back to the living room. She could figure that out later.

"Wow, that was quick," said Amy, peering curiously at Morgan's outfit as she pulled on her coat.

"Don't you look pretty," said Grandma. "You girls have fun now."

Morgan thought that was probably unlikely. She did like Miss McPhearson, but the old woman could be moody sometimes. And it would probably set her off if her young guests arrived late. But fortunately, they made it on time. Cara, Miss McPhearson's housekeeper and Amy's friend, answered the door and took them to the parlor. "May I take your coats?" she asked. As the other girls gave her their coats, Morgan slipped the purple socks from her pocket and rolled them up and hid them in her hand. Maybe it was silly to give Miss McPhearson socks. She didn't even know if they would fit. But it was too late to put them back in her coat pocket because Cara was taking their coats away.

"Welcome," said Miss McPhearson as she entered the room. "Please, have a seat."

The three girls sat down and, as usual, Miss McPhearson directed most of her conversation to Amy. Amy was the one who originally befriended the lonely old woman. But the other girls had gotten to know her as well. And as odd as it might seem to someone who didn't get it, they all got along fairly well. At least as long as the girls minded their manners. Miss McPhearson was a stickler for manners. Sometimes Morgan thought the purpose of their visits and teas was so that she could turn them all into little ladies. Still, it was interesting, and Miss McPhearson's house, set high on a bluff overlooking the ocean, was like a museum full of interesting old stories.

"What's that in your hand, Morgan?" Miss McPhearson asked as Amy poured the tea.

Morgan swallowed. "I, uh, I brought something for you, Miss McPhearson."

"Well, what is it?" the old woman said impatiently.

"Something I made," explained Morgan. "But I'm not sure they're the right size. I wasn't really thinking."

Miss McPhearson held out her hand, and Morgan set the pair of socks in it. "What is this?"

"They're socks," said Morgan. "Polar fleece socks. I made some for my grandma, and she really liked them. I thought you might like them too."

Miss McPhearson unrolled the socks and held them out to examine them. "Very interesting, Morgan. Thank you very much."

"You're welcome."

Then Miss McPhearson set the bright purple socks aside in a way that made Morgan think it had probably been a mistake after all. "Where are the other girls?" she asked. "Emily and Chelsea?" Amy explained about the ski trip, and Miss McPhearson immediately launched into a colorful story about the first time she and her family went skiing, up at the very same lodge, and how she broke her leg on the very first run. "I never skied again."

Morgan just hoped that wouldn't be the case with Emily. Or Chelsea, for that matter. She shot up a little prayer for both of them to come home safely and in one piece.

chapter six

Morgan missed Emily at church on Sunday. And although she sat with Mom and Grandma, she felt lonely. It seemed wrong not having Emily there, not sitting up in the front pew together. And it didn't feel right having a whole Sunday afternoon without Emily, and without having a meeting at the clubhouse since Amy was working and Carlie was watching her brothers. But Morgan used the afternoon to sew up more socks. By the time Mom told her to go to bed, she had ten pairs completely finished.

"Can you sell these in your store?" Morgan asked her mom.

Mom examined a pair of red and green socks. "I don't see why not. Can you think of a way to connect them together so the pairs don't get mixed up? Maybe make a tag with the size and the price on it?"

"Sure."

The next morning, Morgan got up early and made tags for her socks. She sewed a piece of yarn to connect the socks and the tags. Then she emptied her scarf basket and filled it with the ten pairs of socks. By the time she finished, she thought the whole thing looked very professional.

"Here you go, Mom," she said as she handed over the basket.

"I'll put it by the cash register," Mom promised. "People seem to notice things up there."

"Do you think eight dollars a pair is too much?"

Mom considered this. "I guess we'll find out."

Morgan hurried to finish her breakfast and then gathered up her things for school and was just going out the door when Grandma asked why she was going so early.

"I just wanted some extra time to see Emily," said Morgan. "I want to hear about the ski trip without having everyone else around."

Grandma smiled. "Oh, yes. I see."

It was drizzling outside, so Morgan pulled on her hood and jogged over to Emily's house, knocking loudly on the door.

"Oh, hi, Morgan," said Mrs. Adams. "Emily's not here."

Morgan frowned. "Where is she? Did she get hurt snowboarding?"

Mrs. Adams laughed. "No, but they got home so late last night, Emily spent the night at Chelsea's."

"Oh."

"Sorry. But you'll see her at school."

"Yeah …"

Morgan trudged back home.

"What's wrong?" asked Grandma when Morgan went back into the house and dumped her backpack by the front door.

"Nothing…" Morgan stood near the door, just staring at her somewhat soggy reflection in the hallway mirror. Her glasses were splattered with rain, and her beaded braids looked droopier than usual.

Grandma came over and stood behind her. "Is something wrong with Emily? Is she sick or hurt?"

"She spent the night at Chelsea's," said Morgan sadly.

"Oh." Grandma nodded as she fingered one of Morgan's beaded braids. "And you're feeling bad?"

"I guess…" Morgan turned and looked at Grandma. "Do you think I should lose the braids?"

"What?" Grandma blinked.

"My beaded braids. I was thinking maybe I'm too old for them now."

Grandma smiled. "Well, I think that's up to you, dear."

"I think I want to have normal hair now. You know, like my friends."

Grandma nodded. "Well, I'm sure that can be arranged."

"Maybe I can use some of my sock money to do that," said Morgan eagerly. "I mean I don't know how much it'll cost … but I think it will be worth it." Then she pointed to her glasses. "And maybe I should get contacts too."

Grandma frowned. "Why are you so interested in changing yourself, Morgan?"

"I don't know."

"Is it because you're worried about Emily?" asked Grandma. "You think she might like Chelsea more than she likes you? You think that changing yourself will make a difference?"

Morgan shrugged. "I think I'm just tired of looking like this all the time. I think it's time for a change."

"Well, as long as you're doing it for the right reasons ..."

"Doing what for the right reasons?" asked Mom as she came out of her bedroom dressed for work.

So Morgan explained her idea for changing her hair and getting contacts. Mom blinked in surprise. "Wow, that's a lot to change all at once. And getting your curls relaxed and getting contacts won't be cheap."

Morgan pointed to her sock basket. "But I could use some of my sock money. And I could buy more fabric and make more socks."

Mom grinned. "You certainly are industrious."

"So, do you think I could do that?"

"Is that what you really want?" asked Mom.

Morgan nodded eagerly. "Yeah, I do."

"Well, let me give Crystal a call and see if she can get you scheduled for hair. As far as the contacts go, why don't you give that a little more thought, Morgan?"

So Morgan agreed. Then, since it was raining even harder now, Mom offered to give her and her friends a lift to school. And as Morgan rode in the front, with Carlie and

Amy in the back, she imagined how she would look with her new hair. Her plan was to keep her mini makeover a complete secret. Even from Emily. She would surprise everyone.

"There's Chelsea's car," said Carlie as Mom pulled up in front of the school. And soon all five friends were clustered together in front of their lockers. Chelsea and Emily were telling the others about the spectacular time they had riding the slopes, and how they even met some cute boys who thought they were in high school, and how they'd both gotten really good at snowboarding.

"We had a nice time at Miss McPhearson's on Saturday," said Amy, as if that could compete with Chelsea and Emily's weekend. Then the warning bell was ringing, and they all headed off to their first class.

"I can't wait until the ski trip," Emily told Morgan on their way to English. "It's going to be totally awesome."

"I started sewing socks," said Morgan. "It's not very hard, once you figure it out, and I think it'll be a good way to make money for the ski trip."

"I have a plan for making money too," said Emily.

"What's that?"

"Babysitting."

"Babysitting?"

"Yeah, Mrs. Landers has some friends who wanted someone to watch their kids while they go to a Christmas party next Saturday night. I guess it's supposed to last until really late. Mrs. Landers said I could make a lot of money in just one night. She said it might be close to a hundred dollars if the parents tip me. And the kids will mostly be sleeping."

"I didn't know you liked to babysit."

"I used to babysit sometimes ... before we moved here."

"Oh."

"Anyway, it's all set," said Emily as they went into English.

"Cool," said Morgan. Although she really thought it stunk. She had hoped that she and Emily could do the sock project together. She had imagined them taking turns cutting and sewing, then selling them together at the bazaar. Now it looked like Emily had a completely different plan. A plan that didn't include Morgan. Still, Morgan knew that she should be happy for her friend. This meant that Emily would for sure be able to do the ski trip. Unless the babysitting thing didn't work out. Making a hundred dollars in one night did sound pretty farfetched. Besides, that was only half of what Emily needed.

Morgan glanced over at Emily, as they sat across from each other in English. It seemed like something had changed about her. Oh, she had the same blonde hair, same blue eyes, same petite frame, but something was different. Then it hit Morgan. Of course, she was wearing Chelsea's clothes. Not only that, but she seemed to be sitting up straighter. Like she had some new sense of confidence. Was it because she was dressed like Chelsea? Or was it something more? Just then, Morgan noticed Mrs. Robertson giving her a warning look, and Morgan knew it was time to pay attention.

Morgan tried to put worrisome thoughts about Emily out of her mind during her morning classes. So what if Emily and Chelsea were friends. Morgan was their friend too. Besides, Morgan still had Amy and Carlie. And they had their clubhouse. Maybe Morgan should plan a meeting for this afternoon.

"We need to try on our elf costumes today," said Chelsea as the five girls sat together for lunch. "That way if we need to alter any of them, there will be time to get it done before Saturday."

"Want to do it at the clubhouse?" suggested Morgan. "I thought maybe we should have a meeting today anyway."

"No," said Chelsea. "I think you should come out to my house this afternoon. There's more room to try stuff on there. Besides, I think my mom wants to see us dressed up. In fact, I'll call her and tell her to order some pizza. And she can give us a ride after school. How's that sound?"

Everyone, except Morgan, thought that was a great plan. And Morgan didn't let on that she wasn't overly thrilled. She wished they could meet at the clubhouse — that things could be the way they had been. But already, Chelsea was letting everyone use her phone to call their parents and make sure it was okay to go home with Chelsea after school.

"Your turn," said Chelsea, handing Morgan the phone.

Morgan dialed her home number and waited for Grandma to answer.

"I'm so glad you called, honey," said Grandma happily. "Your mom called a while ago and it looks like Crystal can get you in for your hair today. I'll pick you up after school and take you over."

"That's great," said Morgan. "See ya then." She hung up and handed the phone back to Chelsea. Then, putting on a disappointed face, she said. "It looks like I can't make it this afternoon."

"Why not?" demanded Chelsea.

"I have an appointment. My grandma has to pick me up right after school."

"But I thought you were going to help us redesign the elf outfits, Morgan," said Chelsea.

"Yeah," said Emily. "You're really good at that."

Morgan considered this. In a way it was both flattering and encouraging. "Well, could we do the fitting tomorrow instead?"

Chelsea frowned. "I guess …"

"I can't," said Carlie. "I promised Mom I'd watch the boys."

"I'm out too," said Amy. "I have to work."

"Well, what if I came over after my appointment?" suggested Morgan. "Although it might be late … like around five or so."

"That's okay with me," said Chelsea. "We can just hang until you get there."

"Maybe we'll even save some pizza for you," teased Emily.

So it was settled. And Morgan thought maybe it was a good plan after all. She could show up with her cool new hair and surprise everyone at once. It was hard to concentrate on school during the afternoon. Morgan kept wondering what her new hair was going to look like. And what would it feel like? And what if something went wrong? Finally, during math, she realized that worrying wasn't doing her one bit of good. So she shot up a quick prayer. It didn't seem like too much to ask. God could help to make sure that her hair turned out okay.

"How are you feeling?" Morgan asked Grandma when she got into the car.

"Oh, so-so …"

"I hope it's not wearing you out to take me to —"

"No, no … driving isn't a problem at all. And Cleo said to just drop you off and you can walk over to the shop when you're done and ride home with your mom."

"No problem."

"Good luck," said Grandma as she pulled in front of Crystal's salon. "I hope it's all that you want it to be."

Morgan crossed her fingers. Then she told Grandma that she'd already prayed about it. Then Grandma waved and drove away. Still, Morgan felt a little uneasy as she walked into the salon.

"Hey, Morgan," said Crystal. "I hear you want a new do."

Morgan nodded as she removed her coat. "Do you think it'll look good?"

Crystal patted Morgan on the back. "You're such a cutie that I think anything would look good on you."

"I don't want to see it," said Morgan as she got into the chair. "Not until you're all done."

"Deal."

chapter seven

Morgan's eyes got big as she looked at her reflection in the mirror. "Is that really me?" she asked, feeling slightly horrified at the balloon of dark brown hair encircling her head. It was such a change after the beaded braids.

"Don't worry," said Crystal, "the curls should continue to relax."

Morgan nodded, but didn't feel convinced.

"Your mom already paid me, so you're free to go." Crystal handed her a bottle of something. "Put some of this on before you go to bed. Not too much. Read the directions."

Morgan stuffed the bottle into her backpack and glanced at her watch. She suddenly remembered her promise to join her friends at Chelsea's house. Now she wasn't so sure. She wished she had a hat to put on, something to flatten out her really big hair. But she thanked Crystal and headed over to Mom's shop.

"Oh, my," said Mom when Morgan walked in. "You look so different, Morgan." She came over to see it close up. "Do you like it?"

Morgan frowned. "I'm not sure. The curl is supposed to relax more."

Mom nodded as she gave Morgan's curls a squeeze. "Yes, that's how mine is after I get it done too."

"Oh, Morgan!" squealed Maureen, the high school girl that Mom had just hired to help out part-time during the holidays. "Look at you, girlfriend."

Morgan rolled her eyes and let out a groan.

"No, it's cute," said Maureen. "I like it."

"Thanks." Morgan turned to Mom. "I'm supposed to go to Chelsea's to try on our costumes for the parade. Can you give me a ride?"

"You're going to be in the parade?" asked Maureen.

"Yeah … we're going to be elves."

Maureen laughed. "Well, you'll be a cute elf, Morgan. Hope you can keep that hat on with all that hair."

Morgan was silent as Mom drove her up to Chelsea's house.

"You're not sorry you did it, are you?" asked Mom when she pulled into the driveway.

"Kind of …"

"You'll get used to it, sweetie."

"Yeah, sure …" Morgan didn't want to talk about her hair, didn't want to think about her hair and, more than anything, she didn't want to show her friends her hair. She wished that she'd never gotten it changed. What had she been thinking? "Thanks for the ride."

"Call me when you're done," said Mom.

"Thanks."

Then, feeling like a lamb being led to the slaughter, Morgan trudged up to Chelsea's front door.

"Morgan?" said Chelsea's mom. "Is that you?"

Morgan nodded. "Yeah, unfortunately."

"Did you change your hair?"

"Don't ask."

Mrs. Landers chuckled. "Well, I suppose it might take some getting used to, but I think it's really pretty, Morgan. Just look at all that curl."

"Yeah," said Morgan. "Just look."

"Morgan!" cried Chelsea from the top of the stairs. "What happened to your hair?"

"Your hair!" screeched Emily. "What have you done?"

Soon all four girls were clustered around her. Staring and touching and expressing their regrets.

"I loved your beaded braids," said Emily. "I can't believe you did this."

"Me neither," said Carlie. "I hate my own curls. Why would you trade your braids for curls?"

"The curls are supposed to relax more," said Morgan.

"Do you like it?" asked Amy.

"Of course not," said Morgan.

"Then why did you do it?" demanded Emily.

"I don't know …" Morgan felt on the verge of tears now.

"It's going to be okay," said Chelsea. "Morgan's probably right, it should relax more. In fact …" Chelsea patted her own red curls. "I might have just the thing for you. Come on, Morgan, let's play beauty shop."

Soon Morgan was seated in front of Chelsea's dressing table. Chelsea was putting something in her hands, rubbing it around and then she was rubbing it into Morgan's hair. She twisted and tugged and rubbed and slowly, slowly, Morgan's hair began to settle down.

"Wow," said Emily. "That's looking really good, Chelsea."

"Yeah, maybe you should become a beautician," said Amy.

"Chelsea's helped me with my hair," said Carlie, putting a hand on both Chelsea's and Morgan's shoulders. "We curly-heads need to stick together."

"Guess we straight-heads should stick together too," said Amy as she put her arm around Emily. Then they all laughed.

"Thanks, Chelsea," said Morgan as she stared at her image in the mirror. "That really is better. Although I wish I had my beaded braids back."

"You'll get used to it," said Chelsea.

"I'm actually starting to like it," said Emily.

Morgan felt a little better. And soon they were all trying on their elf costumes, which really did need some help.

"I don't know about you guys," said Morgan as she looked at herself in Chelsea's full-length mirror. "But I am not going out in public with my rear end showing through these green tights."

"Exactly," said Chelsea.

"The hats and shoes are cute," said Emily.

"But we need shorts or skirts or something," said Morgan. She took off the oversized felt collar and held it at her waist like a skirt. "Something like this would work, if it was a little longer."

Before long, Morgan had taped together some newspapers to make a pattern for a circular skirt. "Tell your mom to buy enough felt to make five of these in red," she instructed Chelsea. "I'm sure the lady at the fabric store can help her. And get, let's see, about ten yards of red ribbon to use around the waist." Then Morgan took the scissors to the huge collars and after a bit of trimming and shaping, they didn't look too bad.

The girls explained their plan to Mrs. Landers and she completely agreed. "Morgan, you really are good at design."

"And Chelsea is really good at hair," said Morgan as she patted her tamed-down curls.

"I'll pick up the fabric tomorrow afternoon," said Mrs. Landers. "Can I drop it by your house after school then, Morgan?"

"Sure," said Morgan. "And maybe we can have a fitting by Thursday."

Soon the girls were downstairs eating pizza, and Morgan kept telling herself that she should be happy. Here she was with her good friends, having a good time ... but something was still bugging her. She couldn't help but notice the connection that seemed to be growing between Chelsea and Emily. They made what seemed like private jokes about things that happened on the slopes. They talked about clothes as if Emily could actually afford to buy them. Finally, just when Morgan felt she couldn't stand it any longer, Mrs. Landers announced that Amy's sister was here to pick her up.

"Anyone need a ride?" offered Amy.

"Sure," said Morgan.

"Me too," said Carlie.

"My mom is picking me up after work," said Emily. "But that's not for an hour. Maybe I should go ahead and ride with—"

"That's okay," said Chelsea. "Stay here until your mom comes, Em. I want to show you this snowboarding website my brother just emailed me about. They have some awesome stuff and the graphics are totally amazing."

So Emily stayed and the others left. And as An drove them back to the trailer park, Morgan tried not to feel jealous.

"Hey, you're home," said Mom when Morgan came in. "I thought I was going to pick you up."

Morgan explained about the ride. "And we had pizza, so I'm not really hungry." She looked around the living room. "Where's Grandma?"

"Resting."

"Oh …"

"I'm so glad you made that doctor's appointment for her," said Mom. "I plan to take her in tomorrow afternoon, and then I'll stick around to hear what's really going on."

Morgan nodded.

Mom patted Morgan's hair. "Hey, it looks better already. I think I'm getting used to it."

"I forgot to ask, Mom, did any socks sell today?"

Mom frowned. "It was pretty quiet in the shop. But then I suppose that's because so many people were out shopping during the weekend. It'll pick up though. Don't worry."

"I guess I should go make some more socks," said Morgan. "The church bazaar is Saturday."

"What about homework?"

"Yeah, yeah," said Morgan. "I'll do that first."

By the time Morgan finished her homework, she only had time to sew up two pairs of socks. At this rate, she wondered how she'd have many pairs to sell at the bazaar. Or if she'd even make enough money to go on the ski trip.

The next morning, as they were walking to school, Carlie invited the girls to go with her and her dad to cut down Christmas trees on Sunday afternoon. "Dad found out that the Christmas tree permits are only to use for your own family. The trees can't be sold or anything."

"Oh." Morgan sighed. "Well, the youth group is still going to a tree farm on Friday afternoon. Anyone who helps cut trees to sell at the bazaar gets to apply the profits toward the ski-trip expense."

"Are you going?" Emily asked Morgan.

"I don't know …" Morgan considered this. "I think it might be a better use of my time to make socks."

"Last night, Mrs. Landers told me that she might have a babysitting job lined up for me on Friday as well as Saturday," said Emily. "So maybe I should pass on the tree thing too."

"I'm going to pay my deposit for the ski trip today," said Amy. "I don't want to take any chances of missing out."

"I need to go in and pay mine too," said Carlie. "My parents signed the form and everything. Maybe we should go together."

"How about you guys?" Amy asked Morgan and Emily.

"Mine is taken care of," said Emily.

"Huh?" Morgan turned and stared at her. "How'd you do that?"

"Actually, Mrs. Landers paid it for me. She said I can pay her back after my babysitting job. Chelsea was worried that I wouldn't get it in on time …"

"Oh." Morgan frowned.

"Have you paid your deposit, Morgan?" asked Amy.

"Not yet."

"Well, you better get on it." Amy shook her head with disapproval. "I mean it was your idea in the first place."

Morgan mentally calculated how many pairs of socks she'd need to sell to get fifty dollars. Seven would cover it. She wondered how long it would take for seven pairs to sell at her mom's shop. She'd consider asking Mom for a loan, but Mom had already covered her at the hair salon. And Grandma had already helped her with buying fabric. No, Morgan decided, she was on her own now. Still, it was hard not to feel envious of Emily. It seemed unfair that Chelsea's mom had covered for her. Wasn't this ski trip supposed to be about having faith and trusting God to provide? Still, Morgan wasn't even sure how strong her own faith was at the moment. It seemed more impossible than ever right now.

No one was home when Morgan came home from school. Then she remembered that Mom had taken Grandma to the doctor. Morgan prayed that it would go well, and that the doctor would figure out a way to make Grandma feel better. Then Morgan sat down to sew socks. She was just starting the first pair when she heard knocking at the door.

"Here you go," said Mrs. Landers as she handed a large plastic bag to Morgan. "I got just what you said to get." She laughed. "In fact, I nearly cleaned out the fabric store of their red felt. The ribbon is in there too. And I got some red thread and pins and things just in case." She smiled. "It's so nice of you to help like this."

Morgan nodded and looked down at the bulky bag. "Sure, Mrs. Landers. No problem." But as she closed the front door, she wasn't so sure. How was Morgan supposed to create five elf skirts *and* sew enough socks to pay her way for the ski trip? This just didn't seem fair. Normally, at a time like this, she might ask Grandma to help. But if Grandma was still feeling tired ... well, maybe that wasn't such a good idea.

Morgan took the pile of red felt and spread out the fabric all over the beige living room carpet. One good thing was that she could use the whole room without worrying about getting in anyone's way. Then she took out her circular newspaper pattern and laid it out and began cutting. At least it was a very simple design. And being that it was felt fabric, it wouldn't involve much sewing. By five o'clock she had all five skirts cut out and ready for their ribbon waistbands to be attached. The only problem was that little pieces of red felt were all over the rug. She didn't want Grandma to come home and see the mess. So before she could even begin sewing, she would need to vacuum. But before she could vacuum, she realized she would need to replace the vacuum cleaner bag. And when she attempted to replace the vacuum cleaner bag, she accidentally dropped the full bag on the kitchen floor. Just as she was attempting to clean up this mess the phone rang.

"Morgan," said Mom. "We're running late. The doctor sent us over to the hospital for some special tests for Grandma, and it's taking longer than we expected."

"Oh, that's okay," said Morgan, relieved that she had more time to clean up her mess.

"What I was hoping is … could you start dinner? I know that Grandma is hungry, and she had some hamburger thawed out that she was going to make spaghetti sauce with."

"I don't know how to do that."

"I know. But there's a package of Hamburger Helper that you could put it with."

"I don't know how to do that either."

"It's easy. You just follow the directions. You *can* follow directions, can't you?"

Morgan sensed the impatience in her mother's voice. "Yes."

"And make a little green salad too."

"Okay."

"We should be home after six."

As she hung up the phone, Morgan looked at the messy kitchen floor and then over at the living room rug, scattered with streaks of red and looking as if a wild animal might have been slaughtered on it. And yet she hadn't sewn a single sock yet. It seemed like her chances of making it to the ski trip were getting slimmer and slimmer.

chapter eight

Somehow Morgan managed to clean things up and get dinner started before Mom and Grandma came home.

"You go and rest," Mom told Grandma. "I know you're worn out from all those tests and things."

Grandma didn't argue, and Mom hung up her coat and then came into the kitchen to help Morgan.

"How did the tests go?" asked Morgan as she sliced a tomato for the salad.

"We won't know for a few days."

Morgan considered telling Mom about the frustrating afternoon she'd had, but she could tell that Mom was worried. No sense in making things worse. Together they finished putting dinner together, then Mom fixed up a tray for Grandma, and Morgan took it in to her.

"Oh, that wasn't necessary," said Grandma when she saw Morgan coming in with the tray.

"Hey, we can spoil you if we want to," said Morgan. "You might as well enjoy it while you can. We'll probably find out that you're perfectly fine in a few days, and then you won't get all this pampering."

Grandma chuckled as Morgan set the tray in front of her. "You make a good point." She slowly opened the paper napkin and set it on her lap. "So how is the sock sewing coming?"

"Okay," said Morgan quickly. She knew there was no need to worry Grandma about her sock concerns.

"Your hair looks nice." Grandma nodded her approval.

"Thanks."

Then Grandma bowed her head and said a blessing, adding an extra line of special thanks for her granddaughter and asking God to help Morgan get enough money for the ski trip.

Morgan smiled. "Thanks, Grandma. I'm sure God listens especially closely to your prayers."

"God listens to everyone's prayers, honey."

Then Morgan returned to her sewing projects. She decided to tackle the elf skirts first. Her plan was to get them out of the way so she could focus exclusively on socks, socks, and more socks. But by the time she finished three of the skirts, she remembered she still had math homework to do. And by the time she finished that, it was time for bed.

"Did you sign up for the ski trip yet?" Amy asked Morgan as they walked to school the next morning.

"Not yet," muttered Morgan.

"Well, the office lady at your church told me that it's filling up fast," said Amy. "You better get on it."

"Yeah," agreed Carlie. "That's what she told me too."

"I will," said Morgan. "I need to see how many pairs of socks have been sold at my mom's shop. Things were so busy last night that I forgot to ask."

"Are you going to church tonight?" asked Emily.

"Is it Wednesday already?" asked Morgan.

"Yeah," said Emily. "And since I missed church last week, I'd really like to go."

"I'll let you know," said Morgan. "My grandma hasn't been feeling too great. It'll probably depend on her." Morgan had actually been hoping that they wouldn't be going tonight, just so she could stay home and finish up her sewing projects. She knew that was probably wrong, but it was the truth.

"How are the elf skirts coming?" asked Carlie.

"Almost done," said Morgan.

"Good," said Amy. "Remember we're supposed to try them on tomorrow."

"Oh, yeah," said Emily, "I just remembered something, Morgan. The youth group was getting together before church tonight —"

"The wreath-making party!" exclaimed Morgan. "I totally forgot."

"Me too," said Emily.

"That sounds like fun," said Carlie. "Can anyone come?"

"Of course," said Morgan. "The reason for making the wreaths is to earn money for the ski trip — they'll divide up the profits from the bazaar with whoever helps out."

"Hey, maybe I can come too," said Amy.

By the time the girls got to school, it was all worked out. Emily's mom had the day off, so she could probably give them a ride to the church. "Just meet at my house a little before four," Emily told them.

But when four o'clock came later that afternoon, Morgan was still sitting at her sewing machine, finishing up the last elf skirt. And when that was done, she started in on socks. She was just finishing up her third pair of socks when Mom called her to dinner. And after dinner, which Mom had cooked, Grandma announced that she wanted to go to church that night.

"You're sure you're up to it?" asked Morgan.

"I think it might energize me," said Grandma as she put on her coat.

"Sounds like just the ticket," said Mom.

As Mom drove them to church, Morgan tried not to obsess over the fact that she was way behind on her sock-sewing project. She knew that all she could do was to trust God. If he wanted her to go on the ski trip, he would have to make it happen.

"There are only three spaces left on the ski trip," Emily told Morgan when they met in the foyer of church. "And there were a couple of kids at the wreath-making party who hadn't even signed up yet."

Morgan shrugged. "Nothing I can do about that."

"But what if you don't get to go?" asked Emily.

She shrugged again.

"You should've come to the wreath-making party," said Emily. "It was really fun. Carlie and Amy got to know some of the kids in youth group, and it was pretty cool. And we made a ton of wreaths. If they all sell at the bazaar, there'll be lots of money for the ski trip."

"Good." Morgan forced a smile to her lips.

They were in the sanctuary now. "Do you want to sit in front?" Emily asked hopefully.

"I guess …" Then Morgan followed Emily up to their favorite spot right in front of Pastor George's podium. But even as she sat down, she felt none of her usual enthusiasm. And as they worshiped, she didn't feel that old thrill. And that spark that normally ignited inside of her felt as if it was barely flickering at all. She knew that wasn't good. But she wasn't sure what to do about it. Finally, she did the only thing she knew — she silently prayed, telling God what was wrong, and then she asked him to help her.

"Are you going to work at the bazaar on Saturday?" Janna asked Morgan after church. "I don't have you down on the schedule yet."

"And we missed you at the wreath-making party," said Cory. "Where you been hiding, Morgan?"

"I had to do some things at home," she told him.

"Well, we have Emily down," said Janna as she looked at the clipboard. "She'll be working from ten to twelve so she can make it to the parade at one. You could work with her if you want." She winked at Morgan. "I'm guessing you'll have all sorts of cool things to sell."

"Yeah," said Emily. "She's making socks."

"Socks?" Janna blinked. "What kind of socks?"

"Polar fleece socks," said Morgan.

"Cool," said Janna. "I might be interested in some of those myself." She jabbed her husband with her elbow. "Cory might want some too. His tootsies can get awfully cold in the winter."

So Morgan felt a little encouraged as they rode home. Maybe her socks would be a success after all. That is if she ever got enough time to sew them all. She knew that tomorrow afternoon was for trying on their elf outfits again — at least the skirts were finished now. Maybe her best bet would be to kick in the afterburners on Friday. She could stay up as late as she liked since it wasn't a school night. She considered asking Emily to help her with the sewing and cutting, maybe even to spend the night, but then she remembered Emily's babysitting gig on that same night.

"How many pairs of socks have sold at your store?" Morgan asked Mom as they went into the house.

"I forgot to check," Mom admitted. "But Maureen said it's been slow."

"Oh…"

"Things should pick up this weekend. What with the Christmas parade, as well as people counting down the shopping days until Christmas."

"And there's the bazaar," Grandma reminded her. "You do plan to sell socks there, don't you?"

"Yeah," said Morgan. She just hoped she'd have some socks to sell. She was tempted to get the ones from Mom's shop, but then she would miss out on the traffic in town. She was also tempted to stay up past her bedtime to sew, but she knew that Mom would not approve. Besides, she was tired. And she was tired of sewing too!

The next day, Chelsea's mom picked up all five girls after school. They went to Chelsea's again to try on the outfits, along with the skirts.

"You did a wonderful job on these skirts," Mrs. Landers, told Morgan as the girls lined up on the stairway, posing for a photo. "You girls will be the cutest thing in the whole parade. Now let's get you by the Christmas tree." The Landers' Christmas tree was huge, reaching up to the peak of their high ceilings. Morgan couldn't imagine how they'd gotten it into the house. It reminded her that her family didn't have a Christmas tree yet. Usually, Grandma took care of that, but with her feeling so rundown these days … maybe Morgan should take up Carlie's offer to go into the woods with her dad to get a tree on Sunday.

"All right," said Mrs. Landers, "You girls know where the staging area for the parade will be. And you need to be there by 12:30. Hopefully it won't rain, but just in case, you might want to dress warmly underneath the costumes. We don't want anyone getting hypothermia."

"Looks like we'll have to wear our elf outfits to work at the bazaar, Morgan," said Emily.

"Maybe that'll help to sell things," said Amy.

"Now if anyone needs a ride," said Mrs. Landers, "I'm going back to town in about fifteen minutes."

"Not that you all have to leave yet," said Chelsea. "Anyone who wants to hang here is welcome."

"I have to get to the restaurant," said Amy.

"And I'm babysitting again," said Carlie.

"I'll stick around," said Emily. "How about you, Morgan, why don't you stay too?"

"I need to go home and sew socks," said Morgan.

"You *sew* socks?" asked Mrs. Landers.

"They're polar fleece socks," Emily explained.

"Oh, what a good idea," said Mrs. Landers. "I might like some of those for myself."

"My mom has some at her shop," offered Morgan hopefully.

"Cleopatra's, right?"

"Yes," said Morgan. "Eight dollars a pair."

"I'll make a point to stop by this weekend."

Morgan felt hopeful as Mrs. Landers drove the girls home. Still, she felt slightly jealous that Emily stayed behind. It was nice of Emily to invite Morgan to stay too, but it would've been nicer if Emily had come home with them and maybe even helped Morgan with her sock project. Still, Morgan hadn't asked Emily. And why would Emily want to help Morgan when she could stay at Chelsea's and just hang and have fun?

Morgan thanked Mrs. Landers for the ride, told Amy and Carlie good-bye, and then went into her house. As usual, Grandma had *Oprah* on, but she was fast asleep in her recliner. Morgan tiptoed past her and went straight to her room and her sewing machine. Her goal was to get four pairs of socks finished before dinnertime. And then she had a pile of homework to do. She had barely started the second pair of socks when she heard a tapping on her door. "Come in," she called without looking up from her sewing machine.

"Morgan," said Mom in a quiet voice. "I need to talk to you."

Morgan glanced at the clock by her bed. It wasn't even five yet. "You're home early," she told Mom as she turned around in her chair.

Mom sat on her bed. "It's about Grandma."

"What?"

"We got the test results back."

Morgan frowned. "Is it bad?"

"Grandma has some very serious problems with her heart."

"Oh no ..." Morgan felt a lump growing in her throat. "What does that mean?"

"It means that unless she has surgery ... well, she could have a heart attack ... and it could be fatal."

"So, is she going to have the surgery?"

"Yes. Of course. But in the meantime, she needs to really take it easy. You and I will have to do everything around here. I know you've been helping already, but with Christmas coming ... well, you know how Grandma loves this time of year. She gets so busy with her baking and crafts and decorating and everything. But we cannot let her do that."

"Right."

"If it was up to me, I'd say we just cancel Christmas altogether this year." Mom scowled. "I know I sound like Scrooge."

"We can't cancel Christmas."

"I know ... and Grandma would be so sad if we did. No, we need to try to do as much as we can of the things that she usually does. She's already mentioned the fact that we haven't put up lights yet."

"I'll do that," said Morgan.

"And she wants a tree."

"I can go with Carlie and her dad on Sunday and get one in the woods for only five dollars."

Mom blinked. "Really, you can get a tree for five dollars?"

"With a permit."

"Great." Mom actually smiled now. "I'm so thankful we're in this together, Morgan."

"When will Grandma have the surgery?"

"Next week. They're trying to get her scheduled now."

"Is the surgery dangerous?"

"All surgery is a little dangerous, Morgan."

"But she'll be okay?"

"Yes, I'm sure she will." Mom looked at the pile of un-sewn socks. "How's the sock-sewing business coming?"

"Slow."

"Oh, I did check on your socks. It looks like five pairs have sold."

Morgan frowned. "That's all?"

"I thought that was pretty good considering how slow it's been."

"But that's not even enough to pay for my deposit on the ski trip."

Mom stood up and ran her fingers through Morgan's curls. "Well, here's the good news: I'm not going to make you pay me back for getting your hair done."

Morgan brightened. "Thanks, Mom."

"And I'll go ahead and pay you for the socks you've sold. That's forty dollars. And I'll advance you the other ten. I'm sure we'll sell more socks this weekend. In fact, I'm hoping you'll have some more ready for me soon. Your basket was looking empty."

"I'll bring you everything that's leftover from the bazaar."

"Great. I'm going to start dinner now."

"How about if I put up the Christmas lights?"

"That would be fantastic. The lights and decorations are in those red and green storage bins out in the storage shed. You might as well bring all of them to the back porch so we can start going through them."

So Morgan set aside her sewing, put on her coat, and went out to the shed. At least she had her deposit money now. That was something.

chapter nine

On Friday, Morgan's plan was to go straight home from school. She tried not to feel bad when Emily said she was riding home with Chelsea. She knew it was because Emily was going to be babysitting for friends of the Landers. It was business. Still, it was hard not to be just a little bit jealous.

"I'd like to go with you and your dad to get a tree on Sunday," Morgan told Carlie as they walked together. Amy had already turned off toward town.

"Cool," said Carlie. "I think Emily wants to come too."

"Do I need to get a permit?"

"No, you can just pay my dad five bucks. He's already gotten several permits."

"I've never gone out and cut down a Christmas tree before," said Morgan. "It sounds like fun."

"We do it every year," said Carlie. "It's kind of a tradition. Hey, have you paid your deposit for the ski trip yet?"

"I have the money now," said Morgan. "But I'll have to wait to do it in the morning when I go to the bazaar."

"Good. It'd be terrible if you didn't go."

Morgan considered this. "Yeah, maybe I should call the church and tell them to save my spot ... and that I'll pay tomorrow."

"Yeah," agreed Carlie as they entered their mobile-home park. "You should definitely do that as soon as you get home."

"See ya tomorrow." Morgan waved to Carlie as she turned toward her colorful-looking house. Grandma had already turned on the Christmas lights. Morgan was glad that she'd put them up last night. It made everything look happy and cheerful. Morgan just hoped that Grandma wasn't over-doing it. They had discussed everything at the dinner table last night. And Grandma had promised to take it easy. But when Morgan opened the door, she immediately smelled cookies.

"Grandma?" she called out in a warning tone. "What have you been doing?"

Grandma poked her head out of the kitchen. "What, dear?" she asked innocently.

Morgan looked to see racks of sugar cookies cooling and shook her finger at her grandmother. "You're not supposed to be doing things like this."

Grandma smiled sheepishly. "I just couldn't help myself."

"But Mom said —"

"I know, I know, but I was feeling really spunky. And I had a hankering for some good sugar cookies."

Morgan looked at the messy kitchen and then took Grandma by the arm. "Okay, I promise not to tell Mom if you go and sit down for the rest of the day."

"What about the —"

"I'll clean it up, Grandma. You just go and rest, okay?"

"Well, I guess I can't argue," said Grandma.

"No, you can't."

"I was going to freeze some of those," said Grandma, "to decorate later."

"So how do I do that?" asked Morgan as she helped Grandma to her chair where Grandma gave her step-by-step directions. "That sounds pretty simple," said Morgan. "Anything else?"

"Well, I was hankering after a cup of tea."

"I'll make it," said Morgan firmly. "You just stay here and sit. *Please.*"

Grandma chuckled. "Yes, dear. Whatever you say, dear."

Then Morgan made Grandma some tea and began to clean up the kitchen. By the time everything was cleaned up and put away, it was after four o'clock, and Grandma was happily watching *Oprah*.

"Thank you, honey," she called out as Morgan went to her room.

Morgan looked at the pile of unsewn socks and then at the clock. If she could manage to sew two pairs an hour, she would have them all finished by eleven o'clock. That was if she didn't take any breaks, which wasn't likely. Just the same, it seemed possible, and she set to work. Still, it was slow going. Using the stretchy knit stitch was time consuming. But not using it would ruin the socks. Morgan thought about people in other countries as she sewed. She'd heard stories of children who were forced to work for long hours every day in sweat shops, where they were paid only pennies per hour. At least that wasn't the case with her. Still, the sooner she ended this project the happier she would be. She had always enjoyed sewing and creating, but doing the same thing over and over again was incredibly boring. At least the sock fabric patterns were different.

Morgan sewed until six o'clock, when Mom arrived home with Chinese takeout from Asian Gardens. "Amy said to tell you hi," Mom said as she set the white boxes out on the table. "Boy, were they busy tonight."

"That should make Amy happy," said Morgan. "More tips."

"Are you girls all set for the parade?" asked Grandma. Then Morgan told them about yesterday's fitting and how the elf outfits looked pretty good.

"And how are your socks coming?" asked Mom.

"If I stick with it, I should have them all done in time for the bazaar tomorrow."

"And then you'll bring me what's left?"

"Hopefully there won't be any left," said Morgan with a grin.

After they finished eating, Mom excused Morgan to return to her sewing. "I'll handle cleanup tonight," she told her as she tossed a carton into the trash.

So Morgan returned to sewing. Thanks to things like broken needles, running out of thread, or silly mistakes, it was taking longer than her time estimate. Yet, she was determined not to quit until she was done. It was past midnight when she finally finished the last sock. She turned off the light on the sewing machine and let out a big sigh. Sure, it was hard, but she was done. And hopefully these socks would sell like hotcakes, and she would make enough money in one day to pay for the ski trip and then some.

"Time to get up," called Mom the next morning.

"Huh?" Morgan blinked blurry eyes toward the clock. "Isn't it Saturday?"

"You asked me to wake you up before nine," said Mom.

"Oh, yeah," said Morgan, jumping out of bed. "The bazaar. Can I still get a ride with you?"

"If you can be ready in twenty minutes."

"Yeah, sure." Morgan was already pulling off her pajamas and reaching for her elf costume.

"How is the Queen of Socks?" asked Grandma, poking her head in the doorway.

"All done," said Morgan as she tugged on her tights. "But I haven't had time to make tags or anything."

Grandma came over to look at the pile of socks. "You do nice work, Morgan. Say, maybe I could safety pin the pairs together. Would that help?"

"That'd be awesome," said Morgan as she put on a red turtleneck to wear under the elf costume.

While Morgan dressed and ate a quick breakfast of a banana and milk, Grandma managed to safety pin all the pairs of socks together then put them in a large plastic bag. "Now, maybe you can just make a sign that says eight dollars a pair, and you'll be good to go."

"Great idea." Morgan was stuffing her elf shoes and hat into her backpack. "Thanks, Grandma!"

Grandma frowned. "I just wish I could work at the bazaar today."

"Mother," said Morgan's mom in a stern voice as she pulled on her cape. "We discussed this already. You really must take it easy. There's some leftover Chinese food in the fridge. And I do not want you to do anything except sit in your chair, watch TV, and knit."

"Am I allowed to read?"

"Yes."

Then Morgan and Mom kissed Grandma good-bye and went on their way. Morgan felt sorry for Grandma being stuck at home, but under the circumstances, it seemed the only option.

"I can go home after the Christmas parade," said Morgan. "To be with Grandma, I mean."

"Oh, that would be nice, sweetie. I know she feels bad about missing out on things. Maybe you could tell her how everything went."

"Sure."

Then Mom dropped Morgan at the church. "I'll see you at the Christmas parade," she told her, holding up her camera. "I'm going to close the shop while it's going."

Morgan waved and ran into the church. She headed straight for the office, pulling out her registration form and deposit money. Distracted with cleaning up Grandma's baking mess, she'd forgotten to call yesterday.

"Can I help you?" asked a woman that Morgan didn't recognize.

"Where's Mrs. Albert?" asked Morgan.

"She'll be in later," said the woman.

"Oh." Morgan laid her registration form on the counter and started looking for her money. "I'm registering for the middle-school ski trip."

The woman frowned. "I'm sorry, but that's all full now."

Morgan just stared at her. "Completely full?"

"Yes. And we actually have a waiting list."

"A waiting list?"

The woman nodded. "I don't know if Cory and Janna can take any more kids or not, but I thought it wouldn't hurt to take names." She looked at her paper. "You'll be number three on it."

"Oh ..."

"Your name?"

"Uh, Morgan. Morgan Evans."

"Oh, you're Cleo's daughter. Of course." She wrote down the name. "Well, hopefully they'll be able to squeeze a few more in."

Morgan nodded. "Yeah, hopefully." But as she walked through the foyer and on toward the bazaar area, she felt numb. She couldn't believe that she had worked past midnight last night just to sew all these stupid socks, and now she wouldn't even be able to go on the ski trip. What was the point of even selling her socks in here today? All the money made at the bazaar was either to pay their way or to donate to the church's outreach fund. Not that she didn't want to contribute to the outreach fund, but she had twenty pairs of socks in her bag. That was equal to $160. Combined with her fifty dollar deposit, which she had tucked back into her backpack, that would've been more than enough to cover her spot. But now she had no spot.

She blinked back tears as she walked through the sanctuary, which was now serving as the shopping area. Friends from church smiled at her elf costume and said hello to her. She tried to be friendly back, but it was just too hard. Everything felt way too hard. Finally, she got to the youth-group booth, and she knew what she would do. She would donate some of her socks to be used for the outreach fund or whatever. And then she would excuse herself from working there. She would tell them that her grandmother was ill, and that was true — totally true. And then she would walk back home and spend the morning with Grandma.

"Hey, Elf Morgan," called out Emily with a happy smile.

"Hey, Elf Emily," said Morgan, forcing a smile.

"What's the matter?" asked Emily.

"Nothing."

Emily shook her head. "No, I can tell something's wrong, Morgan." She pulled Morgan aside. "What is it?"

"Look, Em," said Morgan quickly. "I can't work here today and —"

"But you have to —"

"No," said Morgan firmly. "My grandma is sick and I need to go —"

"Grandma is sick?" said Emily with concern. "Is it serious?"

"It's her heart."

"Oh no!"

"Anyway, she's going to have surgery next week. And she's not supposed to overdo it or anything … and I just feel like I should go home and —" Then Morgan began to cry.

"Oh, Morgan," said Emily, wrapping her arms around her and hugging her tightly. "I'm so sorry. Do you want me to come with you?"

"No," said Morgan, wiping her tears with her jacket sleeve. "You stay here and help." She handed Emily the whole bag of socks. Really, what difference did it make if the sock money went completely to the outreach fund? Maybe that was for the best anyway. "They're pinned together. I wanted to sell them for eight dollars a pair."

"Okay." Emily peered at Morgan. "I'll take care of it for you. Tell Grandma hello for me. And let me know if there's anything I can do. I didn't know she was sick, Morgan. I feel so bad."

"It's okay," said Morgan, still sniffing.

"Will you be at the parade?"

"Yeah. I think so. Unless Grandma really needs me."

"Well, don't worry about your socks," said Emily with authority. "I will take care of everything for you."

"Thanks."

Then Emily hugged Morgan again. "I really love you, Morgan. And now I know why you've been acting kind of different. You've been worried about Grandma." She stepped back and shook her head. "And I haven't been a very good friend. I'm sorry."

Now Morgan was starting to cry all over again. "It's okay."

"See you later?"

"Yeah." Before anyone else could ask her what was wrong, Morgan made a quick escape out a side exit. Then she slung her backpack over one shoulder and jogged all the way across town and home.

"What's wrong?" asked Grandma when Morgan came into the house. "I thought you were working at the bazaar."

What Morgan really wanted to do just then was to break into tears and tell Grandma the whole sad story. But she knew that would be wrong. Grandma's heart wasn't strong, and Morgan suspected stress would only make things worse. "There were a lot of people working at the bazaar," she said, which wasn't untrue. "And they didn't really need me. I left my socks with Emily, and she's going to take care of it for me."

"You didn't want to stay and work?" asked Grandma, clearly suspicious.

"I stayed up so late last night," said Morgan as she hung up her jacket. "And there's still the parade ... I was just feeling tired."

Grandma smiled. "Well, I know how that feels."

"And," said Morgan with a smile that she hoped was convincing. "I got to thinking about those sugar cookies, and I only had one yesterday ..."

"Hmmm?" Grandma smiled. "That would be nice with a cup of tea now, wouldn't it?"

"It sure would. You sit down and I'll get it ready."

And so Grandma and Morgan enjoyed a nice little tea party, just the two of them. And then they both took a morning nap. Morgan felt surprisingly better when she woke up a little before noon. Oh, sure, she was still bummed about not getting to go on the ski trip, but she wasn't going to let that ruin her life. Besides, she told herself, maybe it was better this way. Maybe Grandma was going to need Morgan at home, after her surgery and everything.

"Are you going to the parade?" asked Grandma as she looked at the clock.

"Will you promise to be good while I'm gone?" said Morgan.

"I promise," said Grandma. "Your mother said she'd take pictures on her new digital camera and show them to me tonight. I want to see my granddaughter elf with her friends."

"Okay, then," said Morgan. "Just make sure you keep your promise."

"And you promise to have fun," said Grandma. "You've been working too hard lately."

"Okay," said Morgan. "I will have fun."

"I wish I could offer you a ride to —"

"Grandma," said Morgan in a warning tone.

"I know ..."

Morgan didn't even mind walking back to town. There seemed to be no sign of rain, and the cool breeze was kind of invigorating. But the best part was that, as she walked, she prayed. She told God that she was okay about not going on the ski trip and that her faith was big enough to trust him despite feeling disappointed. But mostly she prayed about Grandma.

She begged God to make the surgery go well, and for Grandma to be her happy and energetic old self again. That meant more to Morgan than anything.

chapter ten

"You're here!" Emily cried, hugging Morgan as she joined the others in the staging area. "I told them about your grandma and everything."

The other girls all expressed their concern, and Morgan was afraid she was going to start crying all over again. She wondered why sympathy did that to a person. But before long she was distracted with getting her elf shoes and elf hat on properly, and then they were all taking their places on the float and listening to Mrs. Landers' instructions.

"Just dance or sing or whatever you feel like doing," she told them. "The music should be fun, and mostly we just want you to look like happy elves." She gave them bags of candy to toss to the kids. "Just don't throw it too hard," she warned them. "We don't want Santa's elves putting any eyes out."

Soon they were taking off, and Morgan found that she was actually keeping her promise to Grandma. She was having fun. It was fun being on the float with her best friends, and she felt thankful to have them. She even spotted Mom standing in front of Cleopatra's with Maureen. She waved and smiled and tossed them candy as Mom took photos. And before long, it was all over — and a good thing since it was just starting to rain.

"As a thank you to the elves, who were brilliant," said Mrs. Landers as they climbed off the float, "I am taking you all out for lunch."

Morgan considered joining them, but she still felt concerned for Grandma. "I think I should go home," she told them as she removed the elf shoes and put her boots back on. "Mom has to work all day, and Grandma is alone." Fortunately, they understood and didn't pressure her to come. And when no one was looking, she grabbed her backpack and headed home.

Grandma was napping, and Morgan went to her room to remove the now soggy elf costume. She hung it up, put on some cozy sweats, and then flopped down on her bed and started to read a book. But just as she turned a page, she heard a crashing sound in the living room. She jumped up and went out in time to see Grandma's TV tray splattered across the living room floor and Grandma standing in front of her recliner and clutching her chest.

"Grandma," said Morgan in a surprisingly calm voice. "Let me help you." She quickly eased Grandma back in her chair and fully reclined it, putting Grandma's feet up. "Are those your pills?" asked Morgan as she grabbed up a prescription bottle.

"Yes," gasped Grandma.

Morgan opened the bottle and gave Grandma a pill, running to the kitchen for water and the cordless phone. Then as she handed Grandma the water, she dialed 911 and waited.

"It's my grandmother," Morgan said, "I think she's having a heart attack." Then Morgan told the man on the phone their address.

"Keep her lying down," said the man. "Does she have any heart medicine or aspirin handy?"

"She is lying down," said Morgan. "And she just took a pill. Should I get aspirin too?"

"Now don't hang up, but can you tell me what kind of pill?"

So Morgan read the name from the bottle, and the man said, "You don't need to give her aspirin; that pill should help. Paramedics are on the way. Is your grandmother conscious?"

Morgan looked down at Grandma. She was lying so still, with her eyes closed. "I don't know." She put her hand on Grandma's cheek, and her eyelashes fluttered. "Hurry," said Morgan into the phone. "Please, hurry!"

"The ambulance is on its way. Just stay on the phone."

Morgan kneeled next to Grandma with the phone still in her hand. "Dear God," she prayed. "I need you to help Grandma right now. Please, please, God, help her to be okay. Help her heart to be okay. Help the ambulance to get here soon. Take care of her for me, God. I love my grandma so much. Please, don't take her away. We need her." Just then

Morgan heard the sound of a siren, and soon the paramedics were in the house, tending to Grandma. Morgan just stood in the background, still praying.

"She's stabilized and ready for transport," said a woman paramedic to Morgan. "Are you the only one at home?"

Morgan just nodded.

"Want to ride in the ambulance?"

With tears in her eyes, Morgan nodded again and followed them as they rolled the gurney with Grandma on it out the door. She sat up in front with the driver. He told her not to worry, that these paramedics were the best, and that it looked like her grandmother would be fine. Morgan told him that Grandma was supposed to have heart surgery next week.

"Well, I'll bet that surgery date just got moved up," he said.

At the hospital, Grandma was taken to the emergency room, and Morgan called her mother from the waiting room.

"Oh, my goodness," said Mom. "I'm so glad you were home, honey. I'll be right there."

It seemed to take forever for Mom to get there, but Morgan tried to make good use of the time by praying. Then she remembered the church's prayer chain and called the office and quickly relayed the emergency. "We'll be right on it," said a voice that sounded like the same woman who had put Morgan's name on the waiting list that morning. "We'll be praying hard."

"Morgan," said Mom as she burst into the waiting room. "How is she?"

"I don't know," said Morgan. "They told me to stay here. They said they'd let me know. It's been almost an hour."

"I'll go ask."

Morgan followed Mom to the desk where the receptionist seemed to know little. But Mom wouldn't give up without an answer, and they waited until an ER doctor finally came out to speak to them. "They're prepping her for surgery right now," he said. "Lucky for her, one of our best heart surgeons, Dr. Cowden, just happened to be on hand this afternoon. And fortunately we have all her test results from last week, and we've spoken to her GP. They should be taking her into surgery within the hour."

"Oh, my," said Mom. "Do you know how long the surgery will last?"

"Hard to say. They won't know until they go in whether she needs a valve replacement or a valve repair."

"Which is better?"

"If the valve isn't too severely damaged, it's usually preferable to repair it. The human body has amazing abilities to heal. A valve replacement can involve some other challenges like anti-coagulation therapy."

Most of this was going straight over Morgan's head. All she knew was that she had better keep praying. And the more people praying, the better.

"I already called the church prayer chain," Morgan told Mom as they returned to the waiting area. "But I'm going to call my friends too."

She called Emily's number, quickly relaying the events of the afternoon. "I just thought maybe you guys could be praying for her," Morgan said finally.

"Of course," said Emily. "I'm going babysitting again in a little bit, but I'll try to pray as much as I can. And I'll call Amy and Carlie and Chelsea and ask them to pray too."

"Thanks."

"It's a good thing you went home when you did, wasn't it?"

"More like a God thing."

"Definitely. Oh, by the way, I went back to the bazaar this afternoon and all of your socks had sold."

"Good."

"Yeah, I'm sure that seems unimportant in light of this."

"Sort of …"

"Well, I'll call the others. We'll all be praying."

"Thanks."

"I love you, Morgan. And I'm going to be a better friend."

"Thanks, Em. I love you too."

The next few hours were the longest ones in Morgan's life. Several church members joined them, and eventually they all went to the hospital chapel where they bowed their heads and prayed. Then, finally, just before nine o'clock, Dr. Cowden came to speak to them.

"It went as well as it could possibly go," he told them. "We were able to repair the mitral valve, rather than replacing it. The rest of her heart appeared to be in good shape."

"That's good to hear," said Mom.

"She's in recovery for the next hour and will be moved to ICU after that."

"Can we see her?" asked Mom.

"Not until she's in ICU," he said. "And then only immediate family, one at a time, and not for more than five minutes."

Mom tried to get Morgan to go home with one of their church friends, but Morgan refused. "I'm staying as long as you're staying," she informed her mother.

It was past ten o'clock before Mom got to go in and see Grandma. Morgan waited nervously in the hallway, hoping she too would get a turn.

"Grandma wants to see you," Mom said as she came out. "But keep it short, she needs to rest."

Morgan nodded and quietly tiptoed into Grandma's room, going over to stand by her bed. There were tubes and wires everywhere, but Morgan focused her eyes on her grandmother's face. "I love you, Grandma," she whispered.

Grandma's eyes opened. "I love you too, darling," she said in a husky voice.

"Don't talk," said Morgan. "I don't want to wear you out. I just want to say that I know you're going to be okay, Grandma.

Everyone is praying for you, and your surgery went really well, and I just know you're going to be okay."

Grandma smiled, and Morgan knew that it was true. She was going to be okay.

"I'm not supposed to stay too long." Morgan reached over and put her hand on Grandma's. "But I'll see you tomorrow. Rest well, okay."

"You too," whispered Grandma.

Grandma was better the next day. She wasn't getting out of bed just yet, but she could talk a bit and listen a while. Morgan and Mom went to see her first thing in the morning and then again later in the afternoon.

"I went with Carlie to get a tree today," Morgan told her. "It was so fun. We went out in the woods, and I cut it down all by myself. Mr. Garcia let me use his saw. Then I dragged it all the way back to the truck by myself. It's not a real big tree, but it looks good in our house. I put it where you always do, but I didn't have time to put decorations on it yet. It smells so good, Grandma." Then Morgan put her hands close to Grandma's face. "Maybe you can smell it too. I think I still have pine pitch on my hands."

Grandma sniffed and then smiled. "Mmm ... it smells just like Christmas."

"It does, doesn't it?"

By Monday, Grandma was moved from ICU to a regular room, and the plan was to release her by Saturday.

"She's doing really well," Mom told Morgan as they drove to the hospital that evening. "The doctor told me that she'll need to take it nice and easy when she comes home, but that it won't be long, probably sometime after the New Year, and she can start resuming her old routines."

"Maybe it's a good thing I'm not going on the ski trip."

"You're not going?"

Morgan realized that she'd never told Mom about her disappointment. It seemed so small now compared to everything else. "I tried to sign up too late," she told her. "But it's okay."

"Oh, I'm sorry, sweetie. But I thought all your socks got sold at the bazaar. Wasn't that supposed to be your ski trip money?"

"I think it'll go to the outreach fund."

Mom stopped at the stoplight and turned to look at Morgan. "And you're okay with that?"

"Sure. That fund is to help people who really need it."

The light turned green, and Mom continued to drive through town. "Oh, I almost forgot, I sold all of your socks at the store too. You'll never guess who came and bought the last two pairs."

"Who?"

"Old Miss McPhearson." Mom chuckled.

"And you still had the right sizes left for her?"

"I don't know. I explained that one pair was a large and one was a small, but she didn't seem to care. She bought them both."

Morgan laughed. "Well, I guess she can always give them away."

"So, do you think you'll make any more socks, Morgan? I know I could probably sell lots of them."

"I don't know." Morgan just shook her head. "I think I got kinda burned out on it."

"Maybe Grandma will feel like taking it over for you. I mean, when she's back to normal again."

"Yeah," said Morgan as they pulled into the hospital. "She's welcome to it."

The next few days passed like a flash. With the Christmas concert and Christmas parties and the last days of school before winter break, combined with visiting Grandma in the hospital every afternoon, and taking care of things at home, Morgan could hardly believe it when it was Friday and Grandma was actually coming home the next day. Morgan had put off decorating the Christmas tree until Grandma was home. Her plan was to set Grandma up in her recliner so she could watch as Morgan decorated.

"I'd be lost without you," Mom told Morgan on Saturday night after they'd put Grandma to bed. They were in the kitchen, cleaning up the dinner things.

"Ditto," said Morgan.

"No, I mean it. And it's such a blessing that you're on winter break now — you know this is my busiest time of year in the shop. I'd be in trouble if you couldn't help out. Although I feel bad to have you stuck at home during your vacation time."

"I already told you, Mom, I'm fine with this. I'll do some beading and make some Christmas presents, and maybe Emily will want to come over some of the time. Really, I'm just glad that Grandma is okay … that she's home."

"You know I was thinking about everything," Mom said as she dried a platter. "God's hand was really on us through all of this."

"I know." Morgan thought about the day when she came home early from the parade, trying to remember what made her decline the invitation to hang with her friends and go to lunch. "You know what?" she said suddenly.

"What?"

"Well, it was last Saturday when I found out that I was too late for the ski trip registration. I was so bummed — that's why I came home early, and that's why I was here when Grandma had her heart attack."

"God does work in mysterious ways, doesn't he?" said Mom.

"Yeah, he really does bring good out of bad."

"And you're really okay with not going?"

"I am, Mom. I mean, sure, it was a disappointment. But I'm okay."

chapter eleven

Grandma steadily grew stronger, and by the middle of the following week, she was able to sit out in her recliner for several hours at a time. After lunch, she asked Morgan about the tree. "It's pretty like it is," she said, "But don't you want to decorate it?"

"Yeah," said Morgan. "I thought you might enjoy supervising while I decorate it."

"Why don't you invite Emily over to help you?" suggested Grandma.

"That would be okay? It wouldn't wear you out or anything?"

"As long as you don't make me get up and dance a Christmas jig, I think I should be fine."

So Morgan called Emily and asked her to come over.

"I'd love to come over," Emily said. "I've been wanting to call you, but I was worried I might disturb your grandma."

"Grandma asked for you to come over."

"She did?"

"She wants us to decorate the tree."

"Cool. I'm on my way."

"Do we have any more of those sugar cookies?" asked Grandma.

"Of course," said Morgan, "You made dozens of them, and I put them in the freezer just like you said."

"Maybe you and Emily could decorate some of them … after the tree."

"Maybe we could put on our elf outfits," said Morgan.

Grandma chuckled. "Now, wouldn't that be cute."

Under Grandma's supervision, Emily and Morgan decorated the tree. Then they decorated the cookies and took a plate out to show Grandma.

"Those are beautiful," said Grandma. "Too pretty to eat."

"No, they're not," said Morgan. "Take one and try it."

So Grandma took a Santa and bit off his head. "This would be good with a cup of tea," she said as she munched. After tea and cookies, Grandma turned on *Oprah*, and Emily and Morgan went to Morgan's room to work on beads.

"Did I tell you how much money I made babysitting?" asked Emily as she threaded her needle.

"No." Morgan strung a bright red glass bead next to a silver one and studied it for a moment to see if she liked how it looked. This necklace was going to be for Mom, and she wanted it to be perfect.

"In just two nights I made $220."

"No way."

"I know, it was amazing. But it's just because of these Christmas parties that last really late, and I watched kids for two couples each night. It was a little hairy at first because there were like six kids one night. But after they all went to sleep, all I had to do was sit and watch TV. The parents didn't get home until like two in the morning. And then they both paid ten bucks an hour, plus a tip."

"Too bad they don't have Christmas parties all the time."

"Well, they already asked me about New Year's Eve."

"Did you say yes?"

"I said, maybe, if I had help. I thought you might want to try it with me."

"What about Chelsea?"

"She doesn't like little kids."

"Oh ..."

"Chelsea's a lot nicer than I used to think," said Emily.

"Yeah, it seems like she's changing."

"But she's not the same as you, Morgan."

"Well, everyone is different."

"You know what I mean."

Morgan turned to look at Emily. "What do you mean?"

"I mean you're my best friend, Morgan. I hope I'm still your best friend."

"Yeah, of course."

"And we're going to have such a cool time on the ski trip."

"Well, I ..."

"Oh, yeah!" Emily sat up straight. "I almost forgot. I was going to teach you to skateboard. Well, we still have more than a week. That's plenty of time."

"You don't need to —"

"No, I want to teach you, Morgan. It'll be fun, and I know you'll be good at it. You just need to practice a little before the ski trip."

"That's the deal, Em." Morgan sighed. "I'm not going on the ski trip."

"Not going?" Emily just stared at her.

"Yeah. I'm not going."

Emily frowned now. "Oh, is it because of your grandma? Because my mom already offered to come over here while we're gone. She isn't working that week anyway, and she really likes your grandma. She was going to call your mom and offer and —"

"No," said Morgan. "It's not because of Grandma. It's because I didn't get signed up in time."

Now Emily looked confused. "Yeah, you did."

"No, I didn't. The trip was full when I went in to the church office."

"Did you talk to Mrs. Albert?"

"No, she wasn't there."

"So how do you know you're not signed up?"

"Because I got put on the waiting list."

"That's impossible."

"It's the truth, Emily."

"Can I use your phone?" asked Emily.

"Why?"

"To check something."

"Yeah, whatever." Now Morgan was starting to feel bummed again. She had already accepted the fact that she was going to miss out, but having Emily acting like this wasn't helping much. Morgan stayed in her room while Emily made her phone call.

"Okay," said Emily as she came back and flopped down on Morgan's bean bag chair. "It's settled."

"What's settled?"

"You are going."

"Where?"

"On the ski trip, Morgan. You *are* going."

"How is that even possible?"

"Well, I wasn't supposed to say anything … but under the circumstances, I think it's okay to tell you."

"To tell me what?" Morgan felt impatient now. What was going on?

"You were already signed up for the trip, Morgan. Your deposit was all paid, and they were just waiting for you to turn in your registration form, which you apparently did on Saturday, when you thought you were put on the waiting list."

"Huh?" Morgan shook her head, still trying to make sense of this.

"And you made enough money selling socks at the bazaar to cover the rest with some leftover to go to the outreach fund."

"I don't get it. *Who* paid my deposit?" asked Morgan.

"I wasn't supposed to say, but I think it's okay. Chelsea and I were worried that you weren't going to make it on time. And Chelsea's mom heard us talking, and she was so pleased with what you'd done with the elf skirts that she wanted to pay your deposit as a thank you."

"Really?" Morgan hadn't expected this.

"Yeah. Don't tell her I told you, okay?"

"So, I really am going on the ski trip?" Morgan stood now with her arms outstretched, she felt like she was about to jump up and down with joy.

"Yes!" Emily hugged her. "You really are going!"

Now Morgan was jumping. And Emily was jumping too. Morgan hugged her best friend. "Thank you!" she cried as she continued to jump and dance around the room. "Thank you, thank you, thank you!"

"Don't thank me," said Emily.

Morgan paused. "And I can't thank Chelsea's mom —"

"Maybe you should just thank God," suggested Emily.

Morgan closed her eyes and tilted her head up. "Thank you, God!" she said joyfully. But even as she said it, she knew that she wasn't just thanking him for the ski trip — she was thanking him for *everything*!

PROJECT:
Run Away

CHECK OUT
this excerpt from book six
in the Girls of 622
Harbor View series

Melody Carlson

chapter one

"What do you mean I can't go on the ski trip?" Emily asked
her mom for the third time. "I earned all my money and I'm
all registered and I —"

"It doesn't have to do with any of that," said Mom as she
jerked a suitcase from the shelf in her closet, dusted it off,
and then tossed it onto her bed.

"And why are you getting that out?" demanded Emily.
"Are you going somewhere?"

"We're *all* going somewhere," said Mom. "I want you to
go to your room and pack."

"Are we going somewhere for Christmas?" asked Emily,
still confused. It was less than a week before Christmas, and
this was the first she'd heard of a trip.

"Something like that," said Mom quickly. "Just do as I
say and I'll explain later."

"But what about Kyle?" asked Emily. "Isn't he going
too?"

"Yes. I'll have to pack for him. He's still at work. We'll
pick him up on our way out."

"What am I supposed to pack?" asked Emily, hoping
that they might be going somewhere fun.

"Everything," said Mom as she pulled open a drawer.

"What do you mean *everything?*"

"I mean everything that you brought when we moved here last spring. And anything you bought since then. Don't pack any of the things that the Evans loaned us. Those will have to be returned ... later."

"*Returned?*"

"Oh, Emily," said Mom in her exasperated voice as she tossed a handful of socks and underclothes into her bag. "I don't have time for questions right now. We need to get moving — and out of here — fast!"

Emily stared at her mom in horror. "Are we leaving — I mean moving — for good?"

"I'm sorry, Emily. I wish it wasn't true."

"But ... but ... why?" Emily felt a lump like a hard rock growing in her throat.

"It's your father ..."

"Dad?"

"Yes." Mom stood up straight and, pushing a strand of blonde hair from her eyes, she looked at Emily with an expression that Emily remembered from back in the old days, back before they moved to Boscoe Bay. "I just found out that he knows where we are."

"How would he know? How did you find that out?"

"I just happened to call your Aunt Becky this morning. I used a friend's cell phone at work, so it couldn't be traced back ... I just wanted to wish her a Merry Christmas." Mom carried a bunch of clothes from her closet and tossed them onto the already crowded bed. "Becky told me that your dad hired a private investigator who somehow tracked us down. She said that he is on his way here right now. So, don't you see, Emily? We have to get out of here — immediately!"

"But why do *we* have to be the ones to run away?" pleaded Emily. "We haven't done anything wrong!"

"I know." Mom sighed loudly.

"He's the one who should be running, Mom. He's the one who's done all the bad stuff."

"I know … I know …" Mom sighed loudly. "There's no time to talk about this now. Just go pack, Emily. Hurry."

"But, Mom!" Emily pleaded with her. "I have friends here. I have a life and I don't want to — "

"Neither do I, Emily. But it's what we *have* to do. I told you and Kyle, right from the start, that our stay in Boscoe Bay might be brief."

"But what does that mean, Mom?" asked Emily in desperation. "That we'll have to keep running and running forever?"

"I don't know …" Mom closed her eyes and shook her head. "All I know is that we need to get out of here right *now*." She narrowed her eyes and gave Emily a look that said "I am dead serious, and I want no argument."

"Okay," said Emily as she went to her room. Tears were filling her eyes as she began to gather her things and pile them on the futon bed that the Evans had loaned to her when they first came here. It was funny … she'd come to think of that bed, as well as so many other things, as her own. Suddenly it seemed as if nothing was really hers. Not her home or her school … and worst of all, not her friends.

"Here," said Mom after a few minutes. "Just stuff your things into these." She tossed several large black trash bags into Emily's bedroom. "I'm going to pack for Kyle now."

Before long, Emily was done, but Mom was still gathering things up. "Can I go tell Morgan that I'm leaving?" Emily asked sadly.

Mom frowned. "I don't know …"

A New Series from Faithgirlz!

Meet Morgan, Amy, Carlie, and Emily. They all live in the trailer park at 622 Harbor View in tiny Boscoe Bay, Oregon. Proximity made them friends, but a desire to make the world a better place—and a willingness to work at it—keeps them together.

Project: Girl Power
Book One • Softcover • ISBN 0-310-71186-X

After a face-off with a group of bullies, Morgan, Amy, Carlie, and Emily decide to walk to and from school together. There's safety in numbers. Then the girls notice how ugly their mobile home park looks. With help from other people in the park, they beautify Harbor View, which brings surprising consequences.

Project: Mystery Bus
Book Two • Softcover • ISBN 0-310-71187-8

The girls of 622 Harbor View begin summer by working to clean and restore their bus to use as a clubhouse. As they work on the bus, they discover clues that suggest someone who lived in the bus during the late '70s had a mysterious past and is somehow connected with grumpy Mr. Greeley, the manager.

Project: Rescue Chelsea
Book Three • Softcover • ISBN 0-310-71188-6

Carlie makes a new friend. Chelsea Landers lives in a mansion and isn't always very kind. Carlie would like a best friend, but will Chelsea fit in with her other friends? When Carlie is betrayed by Chelsea, she learns how much she appreciates her friends in the Rainbow Club. This is a story about forgiveness and accepting differences.

Project: Take Charge
Book Four • Softcover • ISBN 0-310-71189-4

The girls of 622 Harbor View find out their town's only city park has been vandalized and may soon be turned into a parking lot. They group together to save their beloved park and soon meet an elderly woman with the power to help their cause, or stop it before it even starts. But will they be able to convince her to help before it's too late?

Project: Raising Faith
Book Five • Softcover • ISBN 0-310-71349-8

When the girls set out to raise the money to go on a three-day ski trip with the church youth group, Morgan is confident that God will provide the funds. But while everyone else finds a way to afford the trip, Morgan's plans are derailed by her grandmother's illness, school, Christmas activities, even jealousy ... and when Grandma suffers a heart attack, Morgan's faith is severely tested. Will God provide what's really important?

Project: Run Away
Book Six • Softcover • ISBN 0-310-71350-1

Shortly before Christmas, Emily's family must flee when her abusive father uncovers them in Boscoe Bay. But Emily's friends rally to help get them safely back home where Emily discovers that forgiveness doesn't always come easily.

Available now at your local bookstore! Visit www.faithgirlz.com

Faithgirlz! is based on 2 Corinthians 4:18—So we fix our eyes not on what is seen, but on what is unseen. For what is seen is temporary, but what is unseen is eternal (NIV) — and helps girls find the beauty of believing.

ZONDERVAN.com/
AUTHORTRACKER
follow your favorite authors